The
WIZARD'S
DIARY

The WIZARD'S DIARY

THE WIZARD'S DIARY SERIES
BOOK 1

Robert J. Bradshaw

A very special thank you to: Reid for his insightful and honest editing; Sarah for her encouragement, limitless creativity, and love of stories; Lori for her support and meticulous proofreading; and Jody for his keen eye for detail and knowledge of the craft.

Thank you also to Beth, Scott, Kitt, and my parents, Joan and Bruce, for your valuable comments and help preparing this edition.

The WIZARD'S DIARY

First publication date: March 15, 2021

ISBN: 0-9822775-4-7
ISBN13: 978-0-9822775-4-6

BEAUPORT PRESS
P.O. Box 551
Gloucester, MA 01931

www.wizardsdiary.com

1.32

To Lori, Reid, and Sarah
for the year that never was.

"Dear BoB, I nearly laughed today. I don't think anyone saw. I promise to be more careful."

Mistake #9 - TTM

LIFE ACCORDING TO AARGH

Thrundsday the 39th

Dear Diary,

Anyone who's anyone knows there's only One True Spell. And, if I'm being entirely honest with myself, I wish there were more…a lot more.

Sometimes, when I'm daydreaming, I snap my fingers and poof, the hands on the granddaddy spin counter to what is wise, and I'm magically on time (and not late for the umpteenth time). Or, when the world turns orange at the end of the day, I imagine I can raise my arms and float into the sky–drifting wherever the wind has a mind to blow me. It's peaceful up there, hovering high above the unsettling noise and grunge of Mid- dling Street, and I can see the–

"Oh, excuse me. Where are my manners? No, I don't think I would. Why yes, it *is* a nice offer but all the same. Really, no, thank you. You're too kind. I must be going."

Where was I? Ah, yes. Drifting among the clouds…I mean, the One True Spell. It's a tricky bugger, too. I've spent most of my life studying the thing, and even now, it's pretty hit or miss. Between you and me, it's the misses you have to watch out for the most! And, it definitely helps to have a contingency plan.

The strange thing is, even though everyone knows there's only one spell, they never stop pestering us to cast others! It's the authors, I guess, filling people's heads with the most ridiculous magical notions. If only we could do everything they can imagine…

Anyway, people certainly come up with some doozies, that's for sure! My favorite request goes something like this, in a sincere and plaintive voice, of course:

"Please, dear sir, you don't know how hard it's been. It would be such a small thing, a trifle really, for someone as powerful as you, wearing those exquisite robes and such a fine hat. Is that a peacock feather? How beautiful."

They always try to butter me up a bit. I don't mind that part too much, and I'm rather partial to butter, too, actually.

"If you would kindly turn my neighbor into a newt. No, nooooo, not that big. A small newt would be fine. I don't want to trouble you, and I'm positive that would fix the problem once and for all. Yes, that would do it. I'm sure."

Now, there's an intelligent solution to everyone's problems. By the inside of a week, the world would be entirely populated by wizards and newts! Don't get me wrong. I could do it if that kind of magic were possible. After all, I am a great wizard.

Let me spell this out: M-A-G-I-C I-S N-O-T R-E-A-L! There, I said it. I'm a wizard, and I said the words. Metaphorically speaking, since writing them down in you, Diary, isn't really the same thing as saying them out loud. Still, I'm working on it, and I'll get there someday. Sure I will. It'll probably be the same day I fly. Wouldn't that be nice?

What I'm trying to say is, magic isn't real in the popular flash-bang-turn-water-into-wine sense. I know this probably comes with more than a modicum of disappointment, but sometimes the truth hurts. In the end, we all have to suck it up and move on, or as your great auntilee probably used to say, "You can't grab a garble by the tail and expect it to peel your rutabagas." Auntilees always seem to have a way with words. Don't they?

Anyway, it comes down to this: People need to keep their feet on the ground. Live in the moment. Experience the here and now. Take every day as it comes. Settle down and—

"Oops. Pardon me, ma'am. No, I'm sure that wasn't me. Please, put that down. Yes, I suppose we do look alike. We all wear robes, of course.

"Absolutely. I promise to tell him the moment I see him.

"Wrudge, no! Leave it! You can pick something up later. We have to go. The Lord and Lady are waiting."

The trouble is, wizards aren't particularly good at it. The spell, I mean. It isn't that the spell is demanding or especially difficult. That's not the issue. It's that the future can be an exceptionally tricky thing to navigate.

It's like the roots of a centuries-old tree, spreading out and sending its searching tendrils into the earth—all of those fingers branching, and crossing, and branching some more. The wider they spread, or the deeper they go, the greater the extent of their knowledge. Everyone knows there's nothing more intelligent than a tree but also nothing so enigmatic.

The problem isn't getting them to talk. Trees do that all the time. Have you ever been near a tree when it was completely still? No, of course not! They're constantly swaying and rustling—whispering to anyone willing to listen. Trees can tell you everything you want to know if you can get them to focus, but that's the tricky part, to be sure. It's all those branches of knowledge reaching out this way and that.

No matter how hard you try to get a tree to talk about only one thing, preferably what you're interested in knowing, they won't. Maybe they can't? I've never really thought about it. Either way, a conversation with a tree is like attempting to wrangle an octopus into a dinner jacket. No matter how hard you try, there's always one arm suctioned to your sister-in-law.

The last conversation I had with a tree began something like this: "Arvid stubbed his toe on a root, tripped, and landed in the arms of his sweet Joonily! She relaxed, and her face filled with joy as she...On the roof, of course! How vulgar. Right in the ground, you say?...All he had to do was put the penny back... The towering Mount Ardilakk wasn't always so big. Long ago, it was a mere bump in the road, until the year of the Quivering Quake...No one knows where he disappeared to. One day he was here, and the next, he vanished... Then the third guy from the left held his tongue just so, and..."

You get the picture. It's mind-boggling, trying to sift through it all. But if you're calm, patient, and thoughtful, somewhere in that tangle of roots, you might hear what you came for and that, Diary, is worth three gold pieces in your pocket, to be sure! Not that you have pockets, of course, but you know what I mean.

It goes without saying that the trees are listening, too. How do you think they get their knowledge? They hear everything that floats on the wind, but that also complicates things. You see, it's all a story to them and all worth retelling. Therefore, a wizard has to be careful not to take the wrong root. Make the wrong decision, and you might find yourself lost in a world of fiction instead of fact. Then again, that's the eternal quest of a wizard, isn't it? To never forget your C's: Calm Your Heart; Clear Your Mind; and above all else, Concentration is Key.

That way, we can see things for how they are and not how people wish them to be because–

"We don't have time for that!

"Oh no, I don't think so. I couldn't possibly, but thank you for offering.

"You wanted to stop there, of all places? Figures you'd think that looked appetizing. Oof. I might need to wash my mouth out."

What was it I was writing? Yes. Right. The essential thing to remember is that every decision a person makes can have a myriad of consequences. It kind of makes you pause for a moment, doesn't it? The simple truth is; nobody has any idea what events are being triggered by turning left, instead of right–or choosing the fish instead of the chicken at your grandmamamama's Sunday dinner. Spit out a piece of root gum today, and someone might step in it tomorrow. I mean, root gum is nasty stuff, to begin with, but when it gets stuck on the bottom of your shoe, it can eat right through to your best pair of socks. No one likes air conditioning in the bottom of their shoes, not walking on these streets! No question about it.

"Not today, thank you. I must be hurrying along now. Wizarding business to attend to, you know. Very important. Oh yes, very important. Off to tell the future."

I'll lay it on the line. The future isn't as hard to see as everyone thinks, and you don't have to be a wizard to see it. It's not a secret or anything. Call it intuition, forethought, that prickly feeling on the back of your neck, or plain and simple common sense, and you realize that everyone has the ability to see the future. The trouble comes when emotions get involved. That's when people start seeing what they want to see and not what will actually happen. Seeing things for how they are and not how people want them to be? That is precisely what it means to be a wizard.

Of course, if a person is clever, they can use this to their advantage. If two futures are similar, they might be able to steer themselves toward the one they want. This is trickier than people think, though, because knowing what you want doesn't necessarily mean you know all of the steps needed to get there. That's why I always say, "Follow the One True Root, and it will never lead you astray." Catchy, isn't it? Folks seem to like it, and it's true, too! Of course, that doesn't stop people from trying to change the future, and with simple things, it can work out (not often but sometimes).

It all comes back to wizards needing to think clearly, especially in tense or difficult situations. When everyone else is milling around aimlessly like those chickens over there, wizards must remain still and cool-headed. In other words, we can't let the meaningless things around us cloud our minds. We must stay focused on the task at hand. Considered. Purposeful. Implacable.

For example, I would never worry about which shoe goes on what foot. I make sure both of my shoes are the same shape, and I'm good to go! Now that's thinking ahead, or afoot, well, either way, it's using your noggin.

Unfortunately, the future is a bit more complicated than that. Remember those roots I mentioned? First, I have to figure out which shoe is on the right foot...I mean, which is the correct root. Then I have to wrangle it out of the dirt, being careful not to break it or mistakenly branch off to who knows where. Then I carefully follow it right to its delicate feathery end. That's what wizards aspire to do, dig up roots...I mean, follow the One True Root to tell the future.

This is all metaphorically speaking, of course! No wizard would ever get their hands dirty. We're thinkers more than doers, as it were, and this kind of root-following requires a lifetime of study. Novices often find their minds lost in a maze of branches only to return so confused they can't even remember what they were doing outside in the first place. Thankfully, most of them recover...eventually.

I know what you're thinking, and yes, we do get it right sometimes! With the odds so stacked against us, it's pretty amazing that we ever get it right, but we do. That keeps the world clamoring for wizards and our feet beneath us because the worst humiliation a wizard can endure is to be hung upside down by his feet. Have you ever wondered what a wizard wears under his robes? It's not a pretty sight, I can tell you! I prefer to keep my feet right where they belong, on terra firma.

"Poor old Brindlewise. I hope they let him down today. Are those silk?

"Ah, here we are. Well, now, those are impressive! Look at how polished they are. I can practically see the whole world. Hmm. My feather looks quite fine today.

"Wrudge, come over here. You have to take a look at this. Have you ever seen such amazing marble balls? They're enormous. A very wealthy family must live here. Wait, was that? No. It couldn't possibly be."

Some people call us con artists, charlatans, or worst of all, fortune tellers. Ugh. How degrading.

No! We're wizards. And today, I've been summoned here, to this wealthy lord's home. I'm going to help him make an important decision. In fact, it might be one of the most important decisions of his life: where to hang his wife's grandmamamama's portrait. They say a happy wife is a happy life, so who am I to blow against the wind?

Personally, I wouldn't know. A wizard's life is many things, but one of the things it isn't is settled down. Between you and me, I do think about it—putting down roots and all. A babbling brook meandering around a comfortable cottage with a garden around the back sounds lovely. Even a wizard can dream.

Yours Truly, Aarghathlain

Chapter 1

HOW DEEP ARE YOUR ROOTS?

Making an appearance at the hall had completely slipped Aargh's mind as he studied Upper Middling Street's reflection on the surface of the smooth globes. He was fascinated by how the buildings curved and arced across the sphere, their rigid stone edifices bent and contorted by the polished ball's will. Somewhere in the deep recesses of his mind, Aargh felt there was something he should be noticing, but he couldn't quite put his finger on it. In fact, Aargh was so deep in thought that he didn't realize the home's elegant stone door was silently gliding open in front of him. Out of the shadows stepped a slender man wearing a look of utter disgust on his face. It looked as if he'd smelled something horrible.

"Yes?" drawled the man.

He was a striking figure, dressed from head to toe in black.

"Oh, hello there. I, uh, was admiring your–"

"May I help you?" the slender man interrupted, looking down on Aargh with a remarkably unsettling sneer.

The Thin Man, or simply TTM as he was commonly known (because nobody was brave enough to ask what his real name was), had a menacing curl of the lip that was obviously intended to put people off their ease. It worked, too.

TTM knew that if he kept people off balance, it was much easier to make them do what he wanted without having to ask. This was important to TTM because, as a matter of course, he never asked for anything.

He especially enjoyed it when people looked down at their feet and fidgeted uncomfortably. This was precisely what the little wizard, with the nasty rat sniffling around his feet, was doing right now. Disgusting. Had he no self-respect?

"Today is going to be a successful day," TTM announced to himself. "Another entry for the *T of T's!*"

The *T of T's,* or *Tome of Triumphs,* was a small black book TTM kept on his bedside table. That is, if you could call the stool he'd taken from the beggar down the street last winter a bedside table. It had suited his purpose, so now it was his. This was what it meant to be in charge, and most of the time, TTM liked it.

"Quercus macrocarpa! Where are my manners?" the little wizard blurted. "Aarghathlain le Grand, at your service. I'm here to help the lord and lady of the house with their decorating."

A suave wizard had visited from Metropole last year, and Aargh had been very impressed. So much so, he'd taken the title *le Grand* for his own even though it was more than a bit of a misnomer.

Aargh was bowing so low that his hat toppled off, not that it had very far to go. TTM almost chuckled, but he quickly caught himself. He'd been doing so well, too! Luckily, the little wizard was so preoccupied with putting his hat back on that he couldn't possibly have seen TTM's lapse.

Quickly fixing his sneer–and with an even quicker glance down the street to see if anyone had noticed–TTM regained his composure.

"Well, that's ten, *BoB*," TTM said to himself reproachfully. "Let's try to keep it at that, shall we?"

As well as the *T of T's*, the bedside stool, and the mirror shard he used to practice his sneer, there was another small book TTM kept in his room at the top of the stairs beyond the attik. He called this other book his *Book of Blunders*. He didn't enjoy writing things in *BoB*, but it had to be done. If one didn't strive to better oneself, what was the point?

However, he secretly hoped that he didn't reach thirteen again. He loathed having to punish himself for all of those mistakes. What would it be this time, he wondered? Maybe no tapioca for a week? TTM shuddered at the thought. He hated the idea of giving up his tapioca.

Lifting a bony finger at the rat, TTM said, "Right this way, but leave that *thing* outside."

"What, Wrudge? Kind sir. I mean no disrespect, but Wrudge is my faithful companion. He assists me in dispatching my duties…"

…and sometimes, I have to leave him outside. Understandably, some narrow-minded people have a visceral dislike for ro-

dents. They can be foul things, but Wrudge is not foul! He would never do anything untoward when we are on the job or even off the job. At least, I think he wouldn't. I even brush him two times a day to keep the fleas down.

Besides, a wizard must have his familiar. How else could I channel magic? I know what you're thinking, Diary, and the answer is, "No!" Wands are silly toys for kids to cast pretend spells with in their front yards. You know, when their parents are tired of them ransacking the house.

Furthermore, who in their right mind would maim a tree? They're so majestic, old, and wise. The last thing any self-respecting wizard would do is lop off a piece of a noble ancestor's arm, carve it into a shiny stick, and wave it at people. How demeaning! It wouldn't do anything anyway. Everyone knows a wizard needs a living being to channel magic, and, as far as familiars go, rats are very low-maintenance.

As Aargh entered the building, any apprehensions he may have had about taking this job evaporated in an instant.

"Yes. Oh, Yes. This will do. This will most definitely do indeed!" he thought to himself.

The previous night, he and Wrudge had been taking a late-night stroll along the pier when a shadowy figure, wearing a fishing bib and close-fitting jacket, had stepped out in front of them. The man said he worked aboard the *Prosperity,* a particularly well-known schooner. Aargh knew the ship well but had never met any of her hands before. It was always the favorite to win the Midsummerfest races. She even looked fast with her sleek lines, three raked masts, and deep red sails.

Aargh enjoyed visiting the ports on the River Wide. All hours of the day and night, they were bustling with people and things moving to and fro. No one ever bothered him as long as he watched his step and didn't get in the way of the cargo being offloaded from the ships. It felt exciting, being surrounded by so much activity. The port was undoubtedly the place to be.

Wrudge enjoyed it, too. There was always a fascinating shipment to explore or a snack or two left by the fishermen. Often, he would meet rats that stowed away on the ships. Wrudge was especially interested in stories about exotic foods from far-off places, and he was rarely disappointed!

"You're a wizard, right?" the hooded man had asked gruffly. "Who else would be wearin' robes like those in these parts. You should be careful. Loose rags can get caught on stuff. Dangerous thing on a boat."

"I'll keep that in mind," Aargh had responded. He could only see a glint of the man's eyes under his weather gear and wasn't sure what to make of him.

"I gots this cousin uptown who needs a wizard. Lives in Marble House. Know the place?" the man explained.

It seemed strange that a deckhand this far downtown would know anyone living on Upper Middling Street, but Aargh had agreed to check it out. The truth was, Aargh had little choice, being bound by the rules of the Wizarding Guild of the Ancient Art. The first rule stated: All wizards are required to help those who aren't blessed enough to see the future (as long as they can afford it).

When Aargh shook the man's hand, he'd noticed that it didn't feel rough.

"Maybe he hasn't been at sea long," Aargh had thought to himself.

What Aargh didn't know was that a similar figure had been seen entering the Congregational House that same evening, and many things were about to change in Gemini City.

Thinking back to the conversation, Aargh decided the man must have been telling the truth because here he was, walking past two enormous marble balls and entering one of the finest homes on Upper Middling Street.

As he followed TTM, Aargh noted the smooth marble floor, ornate polished gold frames, and floor-to-ceiling mirrors. Aargh could see into what looked like a sitting room as they passed by. It was decorated with fine metal furniture and elaborate tapestries.

"This is unquestionably the home of a wealthy family," Aargh thought confidently to himself. "A perfect fit for a wizard of my stature...well, uh, standing...um, abilities."

Aargh tipped his head back as he walked. This made the feather on his hat look like it was floating above him. Aargh was sure he knew what would be at the end of that long corridor, and much to his delight, he wasn't disappointed.

All of the finest homes on Middling Street had a courtyard, and this house was no exception. It was even better than Aargh had hoped. There was an open space in the center where a gnarled old oak tree stood nobly in the shining sun. The yard was surrounded by many archways that opened into a veranda. This more protected outdoor space was where guests relaxed when the sun was too hot, or the clouds threatened to end the evening early. No one who visited Marble House ever wanted to leave early.

It was undoubtedly true that Aargh enjoyed a good party as much as the next wizard, but it wasn't the food he was thinking about at that moment. It was the tree that captured Aargh's imagination. He couldn't help but wonder how many stories she must know.

It wasn't surprising that this home had a tree, as all Gemini City houses had at least one. However, only the wealthiest could have a fine specimen like this ancient oak. Most people lived in apartments, and although they also had an open area in the middle, it was usually a small common area on the lowest floor. Those spaces were rarely big enough to grow a tree. It was much more frequent for people to keep a small tree in a pot by the door. When it got too big, they would trade it in for a sapling and start over. This was the primary reason people forgot their family's history.

"What wonders she will reveal to me!" Aargh thought eagerly, trying to contain his enthusiasm.

He was imagining traipsing through this family's past, learning about weddings, birthdays, arrivals, and passings. When he felt that he knew the family well enough, he would change direction and discover what the future held for them. It made him positively giddy with excitement.

Remembering himself, Aargh began to prepare by reviewing one of his lessons.

When speaking to oak trees, the essential thing to remember is that although they can be enormous, their roots do not go down deep into the earth. They stretch out from the trunk in all direc-

*tions, often no deeper than the distance from the tip of your long
finger to your elbow.*

Sometimes, retired wizards were invited back to the school
to give lectures on important topics, and that class had been
particularly fascinating. Professor Bristlebrow had stressed
the importance of knowing about the trees you were speaking to, and Aargh remembered every word verbatim. No
wizard wanted to offend a tree by trodding all over their
roots! That was why Aargh always carried a mat with him
wherever he went. He kept it coiled into a tight cylinder and
slung over his shoulder.

Aargh began imagining ceremoniously rolling the mat out
and gingerly kneeling before the tree. Respect. That was
what was warranted when speaking to a noble elder of the
world, and respect was what Aargh was going to give–

"Ahem!"

Aargh snapped out of his reverie to see TTM looking at
him with a stern expression on his face. Aargh's hat sagged a
little under the weight of that gaze, which TTM didn't fail to
notice. Another triumph for his *T of T's.*

"Excellent," TTM thought. He was up for the day. Maybe
he could go for what he referred to as a twofer.

TTM reasoned that if he could achieve two triumphs for
every one blunder each day, he would always end the day
with twice as many triumphs. The thought of that made him
very happy. In fact, TTM was so pleased with the idea that
he momentarily forgot where he was and began smiling. It
was then that he was even again.

"Rats," TTM scolded himself. "Two lapses to tell *BoB*
about. This is going to be a very long day."

TTM didn't realize that no one, not even the master of the house, ever looked at him; therefore, no one ever noticed his lapses. Everyone was too busy averting their gaze and addressing the wall when speaking to him. It was those eyes. Brrr. They would make anyone shiver. And the sneer? That was enough to make your knees knock. Truthfully, people often pondered if he was made of stone like the marble floor. Perfect. Still. Cold.

TTM attempted to put his lapses out of his mind by returning to his duties. With a haughty air of superiority, he announced, "His Lordship and her Ladyship of Marble House."

Aargh turned to see a rather rotund man and a willowy woman enter from a hallway across the courtyard. As they approached, the shifting light that passed through the leaves of the old oak tree made the embroidery of their fine robes shimmer. They were quite a sight, and Aargh was pleased as punch. He'd been right! This *was* a wealthy family, and that meant old, and *that* meant deep roots. Aargh knew he would remember this day for a long time, but it wouldn't be for the reason he expected.

"Greetings," Aargh began, bowing low and making sure his hat stayed on his head. "I am Aarghathlain le Grand, at your service–Wizard of the Spire, Historian and Keeper of the General Generations, and Root-Reader of the First Order. I have spoken with the elder trees of the wood and counseled lords and ladies in their noble homes. I have…"

"Poor Aargh," thought Wrudge.

He'd expertly snuck in a back way by scurrying up the drainpipe, tiptoeing across the window sill, and sliding down the rainwater collector directly into the kitchen. Really, what kind of rat would he be if he couldn't find another way into a house?

As Wrudge watched, Aargh expounded on his achievements, not realizing that the Lord and Lady of Marble House had walked right by him and into the next room. There he stood, bent at the waist, telling the dust on the floor all about his accomplishments.

It was too much to watch, so Wrudge, being a little peckish–as rats are pretty much always hungry–snuck back into the kitchen for a light snack. Was that lamb he'd smelled roasting for dinner that evening? He was sure the Lady of the House wouldn't mind if he popped in and had a nibble.

Now upright, Aargh continued speaking with his eyes closed as he concentrated on his carefully prepared oration. It was vital to make a strong first impression!

"The Lord of Marble House will see you now," a disdainful voice came from behind him.

"What?" Aargh jumped at the sound of the butler's voice.

Looking around, Aargh realized he was entirely alone on the veranda. TTM was standing near a wide archway with his hand outstretched, stiffly gesturing into the room. Through the opening, Aargh could see many marble pedestals carefully placed throughout the space, displaying a collection of the rarest plants he'd ever seen. Aargh's mouth gaped, and he lost what little pretense of superiority he still had left. No nursery he'd ever visited contained such a wondrous array of living specimens.

Straightening his robes and regaining his composure, Aargh strode confidently into the room.

"We must be having hors d'oeuvres and drinks first," he thought. "How refined," but that wasn't the case at all.

"What's your name?" the Lord of Marble House barked as Aargh entered the nursery.

"But…I–"

"No matter. It's of little importance," the lord continued without hesitation.

Aargh was taken aback. He was Aarghathlain le Grand, and he wouldn't be treated in such a cavalier fashion!

"Sir," Aargh began.

"Do you always blather on this way? It's a wonder anyone ever hires you," the lord retorted.

Aargh's feet began to sweat as he came to the stark realization that if he didn't turn things around quickly, the Lord of Marble House would soon be calling for the Footman.

Aargh couldn't put his finger on it, but there was something different about this lord. He looked like the kind of person who got things done, one way or the other, and Aargh wasn't going to take any chances. Changing his tack, Aargh put on a face of supreme interest and concern. He looked the lord directly in the eye and nodded his head, just enough to make the feather on the top of his hat move to the right as if to say, "You are master of this house, and I am here to serve you."

The lord appeared to be mollified, and he continued, "As you are aware, we are redecorating the parlor. We would like your advice as to where we should hang Grandmamamama. She was very particular, and my wife would like to make sure she's comfortable," he said, with a nod to the Lady of the House who was looking off in another direction as if none of this concerned her.

"I assume it goes without saying," the Lord continued, "that we would also like for you to tell us which place makes the strongest impression as people enter the room. Pay close attention to how guests react when they first see her."

Noting the stern-looking portrait propped up against the pedestal closest to him, Aargh responded, "I am at your service and would be delighted to assist you in this matter. As you can see, I have brought my mat."

Moving toward the door, Aargh continued, "I will now ask that everyone remain here while I speak to the historian of the house. We do not want to offend its roots."

"What in the world are you going on about?" The Lord asked in a derisive tone.

"Don't you want me to speak with the tree in the courtyard?" Aargh inquired, somewhat perplexed.

Once again, Aargh got the feeling that he was losing control of the situation.

TTM was watching the scene unfold from the shadows of the archway, thoroughly enjoying seeing the pretentious little wizard squirm.

"Why would we do that?" the Lord of Marble House asked incredulously. "What a preposterous thought! We only moved in last season. It doesn't know us at all yet."

Turning to his wife, he speculated, "It's no wonder he's so cheap."

The Lady of Marble House nodded in agreement.

"Cheap!" Aargh thought to himself, his cheeks beginning to flush with anger. He was many things, but he was not cheap by any respect!

By this time, Wrudge had found his way back to the Nursery, dragging his pleasantly full belly with him. Unsurprisingly, it looked as though things were going south again.

"Oh well. It was nice while it lasted," Wrudge thought to himself. "Time for a distraction."

Trying to regain his composure and speaking with the calmest tone he could muster, Aargh asked, "Lord and Master of Marble House, if you do not want me to speak to the noble oak tree in the courtyard, who would you like me to speak with?"

The Lord unceremoniously snapped his fingers, and a meek handmaid–clearly weary from many tedious hours of service–brought in a tray. On the tray was a bonsai tree, no more than a foot tall.

"Careful!" the Lady of Marble House snapped.

Her voice was so sharp that everyone, even TTM, flinched. If anyone had been watching, which they weren't, they would have noticed a brief flash of self-condemnation travel across TTM's face as he realized he was down two to three and would have to log another entry in *BoB*.

"This is the historian you will speak with," the Lord said, gesturing to the diminutive tree.

Dear Diary,

Although I respect all trees, I do not enjoy speaking to the small ones. I don't mean saplings. They're lots of fun, so light-hearted and bendy. I mean the ones that are full-grown but still small. You see, the tall trees of the forest are noble and thoughtful, and it's pure joy to bathe in the branches of their knowledge.

But when I speak to small trees, it's as if they're trying to prove something or make up for their small size. They like to use big words that I don't understand or talk down to me. I can't get a word in edgewise! So frustrating.

I would rather listen to the booming Hyperion than to have to endure a lengthy conversation with a Bonsai.

Yours Truly, Aarghathlain

"How humiliating," Aargh said under his breath.

"What was that?" the Lady of Marble House snapped, giving Aargh a withering look.

Had he said that out loud? Aargh could practically feel the Footman's rope beginning to tighten on his ankles.

"Ahem. Sorry. I was saying, 'Oh, what a jewel of a thing.' A moment please, while I consult my *Book of Spell*."

From within his robes, Aargh produced a finely crafted leather tome. It was a special book given to him by his mentor on the day he graduated from wizarding school. It contained only one thing, the One True Spell. Aargh didn't need it, but he always thought, "Better give them what they want" (and his *Book of Spell* usually went a long way when it came to impressing clients).

"Do you mean to say that you don't even know the spell?" the Lady of Marble House asked.

And with that, Aargh was sure he would soon hear the swoosh of air as his feet were hoisted above his head. Of course, if that happened, he would have plenty of time to ponder how this day had collapsed around him, but for now, it was time to find a way out.

"I wonder if Wrudge snuck in the back way?" Aargh thought, scanning the room.

Unbeknownst to the wizard, Wrudge was already on the case. He'd deftly climbed up a particularly ornate pedestal and was in the process of toppling a plant onto the floor. The chaos that ensued was a sight to behold!

The Lady of Marble House was screaming about a rat in the Nursery while the Lord of Marble House desperately tried to replant the remains of his prized Golden Orchid. Several handmaids appeared out of thin air to help, and Aargh seized the opportunity to slip out the side door. Out of the corner of his eye, Aargh caught a glimpse of a slender figure, dressed entirely in black, moving with lightning speed toward him. However, before Aargh could even turn his head to look, he heard the sounds of TTM crashing down to the hard stone floor.

"Good ol' Wrudge!"

TTM had seen it all and was ready. Before the orchid had even hit the floor, he'd made his move toward Aargh. What TTM hadn't counted on was a very smart rat who was much swifter than he may have appeared at first glance.

Wrudge had scurried down the pedestal and planted himself right under TTM's left foot. With a little squish and a lot of tumbling, TTM had hurtled toward the floor. The only thought that passed through his mind was: tapioca.

With as much dignity as he could muster, Aargh and his companion exited the room, sped down the mirrored hallway, and slipped out the front door.

Once outside, Aargh adjusted his robes and breathed in the smoke-clogged air of Middling Street. Then, as he prepared to take his first step toward freedom, Aargh tripped on his robes, fell down the steps, and landed with an abrupt bump that was sure to leave a mark in the morning.

Chapter 2

WHISPERS

Aargh shifted his weight and rubbed the back of his leg. It wasn't so bad. Luckily, he hadn't fallen far, and his ego was more bruised than his body.

With a sigh of relief, he relaxed a little and said, "A narrow escape this time, old friend," but Wrudge wasn't listening. He was too busy trying to catch his breath at the moment.

Recognizing they might not be out of the woods yet, Aargh gathered his robes about him. Still as stone, he carefully listened for the Footman's bell. He did hear a bell, and a shock ran through him. He almost bolted for the alleyway but realized it was only the preacher man calling to his flock. In the end, he was satisfied the only sounds he heard were the comings and goings of a typical Thrundsday morning. What Aargh and Wrudge didn't know was that they hadn't escaped at all.

While the lady swooned and the lord lamented the loss of his orchid, TTM sat in his room beyond the attik and plotted. If nothing else, he was a patient man. There was no question in his mind that the unkempt wizard would soon know what it meant to make a mockery of *his* house. All TTM had to do was bide his time, and his moment would come.

Unaware of what was happening inside Marble House behind him, Aargh tried to shake off his humiliating descent down the stairs and restore his robes to a more dirt-free state. As he did, Aargh could hear passersby snickering to themselves and saying things under their breath.

"Serves him right for wearing robes like that on these streets," one elderly lady scoffed.

Aargh knew they were just jealous. He was proud of his finely crafted blue robes, interwoven with the most delicate gold thread anyone had ever seen. The color was so rich and deep that it flowed around him like the waters of the ocean, the gold threads glinting like ripples sparkling at sunset.

A wizard's robes were often handcrafted by skilled artisans in far-off lands and usually dyed deep, rich hues of blue or purple, red or green. This dramatically, and quite deliberately, set wizards apart from the pale polished stone buildings, flashy gilded garments of the lords, and the drab browns of the dirty city streets (not to mention the people who lived on them). The trouble was, standing out could be a good thing or a bad thing, and right now? Aargh had the distinct impression that standing out was the latter.

Being a relatively short wizard, Aargh had taken to wearing slightly oversized robes and a poofy, wide-brimmed hat. He felt it gave him stature, but in truth, it made him look even smaller than he already was. It didn't matter how much he brushed his robes (or his rat); Aargh always looked a little unkempt. It goes without saying that wearing robes a smidge too large resulted in a stumble now and then. Embarrassing? Yes, but when it came to looking the part, Aargh had come to the conclusion that he'd manage.

When he was satisfied that his robes were back in order, Aargh stood up and surveyed the street. "I guess we have some time to ourselves this morning, Wrudge. Have any ideas? Anything you'd like to do?"

Wrudge didn't care one way the other. As far as he was concerned, it had already been a successful morning filled with an adventure and a most excellent meal. There was only one thing that could make this day better: a nice, long nap.

Aargh adjusted his hat and looked toward the Congregational House. He could see Gemini City's finest homes stretching out before him. They were statuesque stone buildings crafted by history's finest artisans and stonemasons. The lords and ladies (or, more accurately, their servants) kept the facades clean and brightly polished. You never walked Upper Middling Street alone–always accompanied by your reflection in the smooth, mirror-like walls.

Aargh watched the grand promenade of high society up and down the street. Couples greeted each other politely, tipping their hats and curtseying, as they strolled along. The only vendors he could see were flower ladies and shoeshines. No resident of that stretch of Middling Street would allow a fishmonger to set up shop on their stoop, to be sure!

Turning to look in the other direction–which was back along the route they had come earlier that morning–the scene couldn't have been more different. Crossing between Upper and Lower Middling Street was like leaving one city and entering another.

Vying for the attention of people passing by, market traders plied their wares. Children and animals ran roughshod over anything and everything in their way, and vendors' carts and stalls lined every inch of both sides of the street. In between it all, buskers rat-a-tat-tatted on metal drums hoping for a happy penny to fall their way. Aargh smiled to himself as he surveyed Lower Middling Street. It was a dirty, noisy, stinky place, but it was home.

Aargh decided to visit one of the farm stands they'd passed on the way uptown earlier that morning. He remembered their watermelons had looked especially refreshing today! However, he didn't even make it past the next block before a strange feeling came over him, and he paused. The discomfort grew stronger and stronger until he lost interest in the watermelons and the high society strolling around behind him.

Aargh didn't see the chicken man darting between the stalls trying to corral his wayward hens or the lady dumping who knows what out of her window. He didn't notice that someone nearby was laughing or that a young man was hurriedly picking up apples he'd inadvertently knocked off the fruit stand. Aargh was utterly unaware that farther down the street, a lady in a colorful apron was calling, "One for a happenny, three for a 'pentce!" or that an auctioneer was bellowing, "Sold!" Aargh didn't hear any of them. He even came close to having his toes smooshed by one of the metal carriages clattering up the street, making deliveries to the people who could afford such conveniences. His entire mind was focused on one thing: a terrified little girl that nobody noticed—not a single person—except Aargh.

She appeared to be recoiling in fright from an enormous hulk of a man. Aargh was particularly struck by the sight of the nasty-looking whip strapped to the man's waist. Suddenly, the hulking man was gripping the little girl by the nape of her neck. Now, he was raising a fist above his head.

"Quercus rubra!" Aargh exclaimed. "The Footman's going to strike her! Right there! In the middle of the street!" but no one heard him.

As Aargh tried to process what he was seeing, she turned her face toward him. Her skin was pale, like a new shoot appearing out of the ground in early spring, and her chocolatey brown eyes were focused on him, pleading.

The gentlest voice he'd ever heard whispered in his ear, "Help me, please."

Time seemed to slow down as Aargh raced toward her. He didn't understand what was happening, but he knew one thing for sure: he had to save that little girl!

A carriage hit a bump in the road, and it appeared to be hovering above the street. Aargh didn't notice. A fish, tossed by the fishmonger, was suspended in midair above his head, but Aargh paid no attention. The entire city was frozen in time, but all Aargh thought was, "The girl. Hurry up! Get to the girl."

It's important to note that wizards don't run. Period. Full stop. End of discussion. All of that arm-flailing and robe-flapping is entirely too undignified. Even when being chased by an angry mob because you told a meeting of the local Farmers' Guild, "Don't worry. The weather will be mild," but then it rained for three weeks straight, resulting in the loss of all crops due to mold–a wizard didn't run. No way. Not ever.

It's not that wizards couldn't run if they wanted to, although few had tried, and even fewer were good at it. It's that wizards are more refined than that. Suave. Sophisticated, even. And running in robes is never sophisticated!

If it looked like a wizard's feet might be leaving the ground without his consent, he didn't run away screaming. No! He opted for a more discerning retreat, like jumping on the back of a cart and hiding under the straw until he was many squares downtown.

This is why what happened next was so surprising to everyone on Middling Street.

Aargh scooped up the girl, and without a second thought, he ran like the wind.

"I've got you," he assured her, and Aargh felt the bundle of robes give him a squeeze.

The humiliation of a second undignified escape on the same day didn't even cross Aargh's mind. And he certainly didn't have to look over his shoulder to know what was charging down the street behind them.

"Not such a bad thing, being small," Aargh thought as he weaved, bobbed, and sidestepped things that shouldn't be trodden on. But then, a trifle of a thought entered his mind that made him zig when he should have zagged.

"Where?"

With a jolt, Aargh realized that he knew *why* he was running, *who* he was running from, and *what* the consequences would be if he didn't run, but he didn't know *to where* he was running. Fear grabbed hold of his heart and started to squeeze. The pain in his chest made it hard to concentrate, and the air around him felt thick as he tried to suck it into his collapsing lungs.

Then, Aargh stepped on the hem of his robes and tripped. A tumbling heap of wizard, girl, and robes collapsed onto the hard stone street.

"Concentrate, Aargh," he chastised himself.

The fall jogged his memory, and an image of his mentor standing over him filled his mind.

"Remember your *C's* young Aargh," a tall man in purple and gold embroidered robes was saying. His wide-brimmed hat tilted down as he instructed, "Concentration is key."

The notion that wizards are angry, brooding, or even crazy couldn't be further from the truth. Popular culture sees wizards as wild or dangerous, always going off half-cocked, but the reality is, they're relatively calm inside. They have to be. How else could they follow the One True Root? And no wizard embodied that serenity more than Aargh's former mentor, Aldenthwaine.

"But it is more than just concentration," the wise wizard continued calmly. "We must control the emotions that fill our hearts and minds, or we won't be able to tell fantasy from the future. Never forget that everyone in the world fantasizes about the future. Call it daydreaming, hope, or even planning, but all of it resides in the deepest desires of our hearts, and all of it becomes a branch of Mother Tree's long roots.

"You see, trees can't tell the difference between what is going to happen and what people want to happen. To them, it's all real. Trees are fascinated by our thoughts, recording them all, but only adept wizards can calm their hearts and clear their minds enough to hear the difference between hope and reality."

"Can I tell my own future?" the naive young wizard asked sincerely.

With a good-natured chuckle, Aldenthwaine replied, "Sadly no, young Aargh. Although, I wish we could. Our own futures are too rooted in our emotions. There has never been a wizard in the world who could see clearly enough to determine their future. That hasn't kept us from trying, of course, but we always wind up branching off to what we hope will happen. That is the burden of all wizards. No matter what the problem is, and no matter how hard we try, we are only able to see the future for others–never ourselves."

Taking a deep breath and collecting his thoughts, Aargh asked, "Are you alright?"

The bundle just giggled.

Aargh was about to lift her up again when something caught his eye. Even though it was only a slight glint in the shadows, he knew what it was. He could see Wrudge's eyes fixed squarely on him.

"Good ol' Wrudge," Aargh thought, "Always thinking, aren't you?"

Wasting no time, Wrudge, Aargh, and the giggling bundle of robes slipped into the shadows of the alleyway and down into the secret world of rats.

Chapter 3

A LIGHT AT THE END
OF THE TUNNEL

Glistening in the bright summer sun, the Footman's brass bell swung back and forth atop its post. Clang! Clang, clang! The bell's sound pierced the din of Middling Street, and everyone knew what that meant: a wizard hadn't performed his duties. Up and down the street, doors slammed, and shutters clapped. Venders covered their carts, moving off Lower Middling Street and onto the sidestreets. There wasn't a single soul who wanted to get in the way of the Footman.

He could be reasonable enough (if you behaved), but to say the Footman was an imposing figure would have been a gross understatement. He stood at least a full head above everyone else in the city, and today, as he looked over the crowd, he was in no mood for fooling around. He'd already lost his first quarry of the day–a little girl caught stealing a loaf of bread from Stall 37: *Bwain's Bread Bakery and Butter Stand*–and he was determined not to lose another. Business had been in a bit of a lull lately, and he was even more surly than usual.

Wizard-hoisting was a specialized craft, and Big G, as he was known to the barflies he drank with, also kept a sideline helping the local sheriff. The sheriff wasn't really the enforcer type; he'd gotten the job because his uncle was Lord of Opal Hall. Therefore, he was immensely relieved when Big G showed up one busy Mundsday morning offering to help. Big G had been deputized in a matter of moments and ushered out the door onto his first beat–a win/win for all concerned. That was until the little girl had escaped.

As Big G prowled Middling Street, he mulled over what had happened that morning. Being more of a doer than a thinker, he was pretty befuddled by the whole thing. One moment he was holding the little girl, and the next, she'd vanished.

Big G began to wonder if the grog he'd drank at *Blunder-Buss' Underground Ale House* had something extra in it. Well, something more than usual, as he knew Buss had a habit of watering down the spirits with carriage fuel. You could really feel that stuff burn when it went down.

Big G had a menacing presence, carrying a thick rope draped over one shoulder and a whip at his side. The rope was a dangerous-looking thing made of strong hemp and expertly tied with the Footman's Knot. Today, as he walked, Big G cracked his whip in anger. It was a terrible sound that ricocheted off the stone buildings that lined Middling Street.

Big G hadn't always wanted to be a Footman. When he was a boy, he often dreamed about designing mechanical things. If it had gears or steam, he loved it. And above all else, Big G was fascinated by the thought of creating a flying machine. Consequently, he often scribbled or carved pictures of himself with wings on anything that couldn't pull itself away from him. Unfortunately, being a thoroughly preposterous idea to Geminians, drawing and talking about flying resulted in Big G being ridiculed by the other children and teachers, so he'd stopped.

As absurd as the thought was, he couldn't give up thinking about how much fun it would be to see the city from the sky. In the end, however, it turned out Big G was better at breaking things than putting them together.

His first job was at school, where he clapped all of the chalk dust out of the erasers. He was very good at it, too, but after being expelled for clapping the chalk dust out of little Jimmy Tiddle, he'd moved into the junkyard. There Big G spent his days dismantling carriages. *Dismantling* was a polite way of saying he pulverized everything with a sledgehammer. It was rather cathartic.

Then Big G got his big break.

One rainy day, the City Footman was preparing to hoist a rather rotund wizard, but things weren't going as planned. For one thing, the wizard wasn't being cooperative. This wasn't unusual but wrangling that mass of wet robes, keeping track of his rope, and contending with the slick scaffold proved to be more of a challenge than he'd anticipated. When the Footman had finally gotten everything in order, he heaved, and the rest was history. His foot slipped on the wet surface, and he fell backward onto the ground.

Seizing the opportunity, the rotund wizard slipped his feet out of the rope and rolled himself off the metal platform. As he barreled down the street, he took a look over his shoulder to see if he was being pursued and that, it turned out, was a mistake. Big G stepped into his path, and the wizard ran right into him.

Without even breaking a sweat, Big G had put the wizard under his arm, strolled the man back up to the scaffold, and hoisted him up by his feet in record time. From that moment on, Big G was the new City Footman. He enjoyed it most days, but not today.

Crack! Crack, crack!

"Where is that little wizard with the droopy robes?"

• • •

A small splash echoed in the silent darkness.

"Ew, that's disgusting," Aargh said under his breath.

He saw Wrudge's eyes squint as if to say, "You're in my world now. Show some respect!"

The bundle giggled.

Whispering with some urgency, Aargh tried to get Wrudge's attention in the darkness.

"Please, Wrudge. We can't see well. Could we stick to places where there are openings to the street? You know, where the light shines down? That way, we could see better. It's so dark."

Something stirred in Aargh that he hadn't thought about in a long time. At first, it was a slight tickle. Then it was a flash of images. Then, the walls were closing in!

"Let me out!" Aargh's voice echoed in the tunnels as he collapsed to the floor. "Please, let me out!"

His arms were tight to his sides, struggling against some unseen binding.

Already racing down the tunnel, Wrudge glanced back over his shoulder. He saw the little girl sitting beside Aargh, brushing the hair from his face and gently saying, "There, there. It's okay. It's only the dark. Nothing to worry about."

Dear Diary,

We haven't met yet, but my name is Aarghathlain. I've just started wizarding school. I was looking forward to my first class today, but I never got there.

Two older boys invited me to see a cool bug they'd found, but when I looked, they pushed me into a box in the school's basement. I could hear them laughing and thumping all the way up the steps. I tried, but I couldn't get myself out. "Let me out," I yelled, but no one could hear me. It was terrifying. Something with lots of legs crawled across my neck. I wasn't able to brush it away because my arms were stuck, too.

After a while, I got so tired from yelling that I fell asleep. The next thing I knew, I was being carried up the stairs, still stuck in the box. When they put me down, I could hear people whispering, and a voice commanded, "Get yourself out!"

"I can't!" I said and begged for someone to help me, but no one did. Finally, I figured out how to move one of my arms, and I was able to push out of the box. That was when I realized it was lunchtime, and I was standing in front of the entire school. They all laughed at me, and I was scolded for missing my first class.

I don't know what I'll write in you, Diary, but I hope it's about better things than what happened today. Tomorrow, I won't look in any boxes for bugs, and I'll get to class early. I'll

*even sit in the front row and try not to mess up again, but I
can't promise. Sometimes, it's hard not to mess up.*

                                    Yours Truly, Aarghathlain

"He's back," the little girl said, smiling kindly. "And he's
brought friends."

Slowly, Aargh remembered where he was. He wasn't back
at wizarding school; he was under the city with Wrudge and
the little girl. As his eyes adjusted to the light, he saw something so unexpected that he once again forgot all about the
day he'd started writing in his diary. Hundreds—no, thousands—of rats were carpeting the tunnel as far as he could see.
They were all puffed up, and a soft, golden glow was coming
from each and every one of them. Their light filled the tunnel, and Aargh relaxed. Once again, his faithful familiar had
saved the day.

"Wrudge, old friend," he whispered, wiping the sweat
from his brow. "You never showed me."

Word under the street was that people were on to the rats.
This was making it harder and harder for them to forage for
food. Wrudge had promised the scared and starving rats that
Aargh could help them. In return, the rats had agreed to
speak with his friend, even though it meant breaking the
most solemn rule of Ratdom.

"Secrecy is security. Secrecy is security. Secrecy is security!"
the rats would chant when they gathered. It was their most
sacred oath.

All rats knew that danger lurked in every corner of the
world for them. If they let their guard down—even for an
instant—there could be dire consequences. Allowing people

into their world had never been done before, but the rats trusted Wrudge. He was a bit of a hero as he was the only living rat to leave the Underoof Collective and live side by side with people.

Truthfully, it was his stories about the food that impressed the rats the most. Living with Aargh was just a perk as far as they were concerned. So, if Wrudge said Aargh was safe, they trusted him, to a point.

The sewer was a maze of tunnels that connected every building in the entire city. If you could master its ins and outs, there wasn't anywhere you couldn't go.

True, sometimes people came down to fix things, hide, or do other people-type things, but the rats were careful never to reveal their secrets. The truth was, Wrudge was taking a considerable risk, bringing Aargh and the little girl down here, and he hoped it would be worth it.

"Don't worry. It will be," the little girl whispered.

Wrudge almost tripped over his own feet. She couldn't have been talking to him, could she?

Giggles were her only reply.

Feeling a bit better, Aargh got to his feet and started following the golden path before him. He was careful not to step on any rats, but he didn't need to be. The rats deftly moved out of the way as they led Aargh and the little girl down a path that was flat and easy to walk on. Aargh was thankful for that as he was still feeling woozy.

It was hard to tell distance in the bowels of the city, but Aargh had a feeling they were reaching a crossroads. The problem was, he wasn't sure what kind of a crossroads. That was before he saw the wall of rats in front of them reaching to the ceiling. Aargh let out a cry that sounded more like a door hinge screeching than a person, and he began to sway.

Piles of rats were stacked on top of each other, barring the way. Aargh's brain couldn't process what he was seeing. There were hundreds of pointy noses poking out of the wall of fur, and the unceasing motion tricked his eyes like an optical illusion. Not being able to focus made him feel queasy. It reminded Aargh of the first time he'd sailed down the river on a ship–especially how wobbly his legs had felt and how a dull, persistent ache in his stomach had kept him hanging over the gunwale for the entire trip.

Every time he'd tried to stand up, a new wave of nausea overtook him, and over he went again. Few things affect a person's mind like being seasick. The one thing you desperately need–stability under your feet–is the only thing you absolutely cannot have.

"Look up!" the hands had said, clapping him on the back. "You've got to get your sea legs!" but nothing had helped.

"Looks like we've got a duffer here, boys. Whadaya think? Should we throw him back?" they'd joked.

No matter what he'd tried, the pain had gotten worse and worse until the world seemed to wobble and spin around him. He would never climb aboard a boat again without having something to eat and drink first–especially on a hot or choppy day!

Just like that day aboard the ship, Aargh began to topple over again, only this time, the little girl was there to steady him.

"You're okay. The floor isn't moving," she whispered.

Slowly, Aargh regained his composure. Somehow, the girl's words were calming and helped him focus. She gently tugged on his arm, and he bent down.

"They want to know if you'll keep their secret," she said, pointing at the undulating rat-wall. It was continually moving as rats moved from the bottom to the top of the pile.

Aargh started to say, "How?" but it didn't matter. He would find out later.

"Please, tell them I won't reveal their secret to anyone. I promise."

"That isn't enough," she returned.

"What do you mean, that isn't enough? I'm a Root-Reader of the First Order. My word is a solemn oath," he said with as much resentfulness as he could muster.

There was noticeable movement in the tunnel as the rats shifted uneasily.

"Shhh. Be gentle. The rats are worried, and they need your help. People have been preventing them from foraging for food, and they're starving. If you're willing to help them, they will help you."

Relaxing, Aargh responded, "I would be happy to help them. They should know that any friend of Wrudge's is a friend of mine."

The wall of rats appeared to melt before them, revealing a large open area with many connecting tunnels. Every opening was filled with rats jostling for position, eagerly awaiting the discussion.

And so, the first Rat/Human congress began.

For a long time, Aargh sat listening to the rats tell their stories. Having a conversation with rats is always a communal experience. Each rat's part weaved together with the last until a picture of what they were describing emerged. Aargh was fascinated. He'd always loved stories, so he felt right at home. The elder rats spoke slowly, with wise insight, and the younger rats eagerly interjected details they felt were important. For hours the little girl translated, and Aargh listened intently.

After a while, the little girl began to get tired. At first, she shifted her weight, changing the way she was sitting. Then she started to lean against Aargh. Then she climbed into his lap.

Finally, when she laid her head on his shoulder, he said, "Little One, it's been a long day, and you're exhausted. We can stop for now and rest. I'll bring you home in the morning. Okay?"

"To your home?" she asked the wizard, brightening at the thought.

"No, to yours. You do have a home, don't you?"

She only looked away.

Aargh thought for a moment and then asked, "May I see your hands, Little One?"

She lifted her hands, and when he turned them over, Aargh understood. This wasn't the first time he'd seen that mark, especially in the lowest blocks. He also empathized because he knew how hard it was to be on your own.

With a heavy heart, Aargh covered the marks and asked, "Wrudge, would you please find out if we can stay here for the night? We have nowhere safe to go."

From the moment Wrudge had brought his friends into the Underoof, the rats were curious about the strangers, but they were cautious, too. Everything they did was careful and deliberate, even when asking questions about Aargh and the little girl.

In the same way they told stories, no single rat asked a complete question. As they passed through the tunnels, the closest rat would start asking something, then others would finish the thought. When they were satisfied with the answer, they would share it with the others like a great game of Pass It On, only the rats didn't embellish their stories. Embellishing a story was dangerous and could lead a rat into trouble. Unlike people, whose stories often got more grandiose with each telling, rats were careful to relate anything they heard as accurately and succinctly as possible.

Unsurprisingly, they were primarily interested in understanding why Aargh came to the Underoof instead of going to his home. And was the wizard's home nice? Did they live in the Wizards' Spire?

"Yes, yes," Wrudge told them. They had a lovely room in the Spire dormitory, and they kept it clean and orderly like all wizards were required to do. Sometimes, Aargh checked the job boards or marked off their duties, but they were out and about most of the time. That was why it was unlikely anyone would have even noticed they were gone. Aargh was a Spire Historian and Keeper of the General Generations; therefore, he was often away, traveling to the edges of the city gathering information or studying family trees.

Now that Aargh was a working wizard, he didn't attend many classes. Still, they did drop by the cafeteria every now and then. Aargh was rather partial to their cranberry crisp. They hoped to visit the bogs one day, but those were far down the river from Gemini City. Few people in the city had ever even seen a cranberry, let alone eaten one. The wizards had them imported when they were in season: nothing but the best for the wizards.

However, they were far from the Spire now, and with the Footman after them, it wasn't safe to travel on the streets. So, here they were, in the Underoof, and they were grateful for that, too.

Wrudge didn't tell the rats that their Spire dorm room was clean and orderly because they rarely stayed there. Unlike most wizards, Aargh liked to be in the center of things, not cooped up in the Spire, forever looking out at the city.

Most nights, Aargh and Wrudge stayed downtown in a tiny second-floor apartment. From there, they could safely watch the city's goings-on and pop down to the ports for a walk or to buy a snack at the many Middling Street food carts. Sometimes, with a minor wardrobe change, they would take a trip to visit a hostel or one of the many shelters that had been appearing in recent years. Aargh enjoyed hearing a good yarn, and there was no shortage of characters in these places spinning one for anyone willing to listen. Formerly only places where wayfarers and deckhands would pass a night or two, shelters were becoming more common—especially in the poorer, lowest squares. Thick red arrows with a circle in the center identified their entrances.

It was in these places that Aargh and Wrudge had seen the little girl's marks before. All foundlings were marked—ostensibly to keep track of them for their own safety, but in reality, it was to prevent them from stealing food in the marketplace. After a night of fascinating tales on the high seas or crossing the highland pass, Wrudge noticed that Aargh always left a loaf of bread behind.

Now, he saw that same kindness as Aargh gingerly picked up the little girl and followed an important-looking rat into a small hole in the wall.

Aargh was relieved to see the space was dry and that the floor was covered with soft moss. It was no fun trying to sleep on hard stone, and he no longer had his mat. He must have dropped it on the street when they fell. It would have been nice to have, but the moss would do nicely.

"Maybe it's time for a new mat anyway," Aargh thought to himself.

He looked around for a comfortable spot and laid the little girl down.

When he started to leave, she said, "Please, don't go."

"Why would I do that? I'll be right over there."

"Don't leave me."

"All right, but you'll have to make room."

The little girl smiled and scooched over.

"Why did you help me?" she asked.

"Because you're special."

"Why?"

"Because you're a child of the trees. We're all children of the trees, and all children of the trees are special."

"Not everyone thinks so. That man didn't think so. He wanted to hurt me."

Aargh thought about this for a moment and replied, "Yes, it's true. The world can be a hard place sometimes, and people don't always remember their lessons."

"What lessons?"

"Oh, Little One. So many questions! I thought you were tired," Aargh said with a chuckle.

Yawning and snuggling closer, she replied, "I'm not tired. I'm special."

"Yes, that's true."

Deep down, Aargh knew there was something important he needed to ask the child, but every time he tried, the words became misty and distant in his mind–like trying to see ships slowly moving with the river on a foggy night. He closed his eyes to focus on the thought, but that only made it harder to concentrate. In the end, Aargh chalked it up to being tired after a long and challenging day. Maybe, after a night's rest, he'd be able to see things more clearly.

Aargh returned to the moment and comforted the little girl, "Rest now. You're safe. I promise I won't let anything bad happen to you."

She smiled and gently reached out a tiny hand toward Wrudge. He let the child bring him close to her, as what rat doesn't love to snuggle?

"Will you tell me a story?"

"Haven't you heard enough stories?" the wizard replied, not yet understanding that no child in the history of the world had ever heard *enough* stories.

"I want to hear one of your stories."

"Let's see," Aargh said with a smile. "I think I have a few to choose from. Mystery or adventure?"

"Adventure," she replied with a gleam in her eye.

And so the wizard began in his best storytelling voice, "Once upon a time, in a magical land, a famous wizard–who, by the way, wore the finest blue robes anyone had ever seen–was taking a walk. He'd recently visited a wealthy lord and lady's home to help decorate their parlor when he heard the sweetest voice whisper…"

As the wizard spoke, the girl drifted off to sleep, resting easily for the first time in a long time, in the peaceful quiet under the never-ceasing clanking of Middling Street.

Chapter 4

A NEW WORLD, A WIZARD, AND A WAND

Inside the tunnels, the rats were buzzing with activity. Aargh could feel the energy in their movement, and he wanted to see what was going on. He gently touched the little girl on her shoulder. Rolling over, she stretched and yawned. It made Aargh feel warm inside to watch her, and for a brief moment, he wondered if he might be coming down with something. No matter. He would worry about that later. Right now, they needed to find out why there was so much activity in the Underoof. The pair emerged from their hole in the wall to see countless rats moving with purpose, scurrying in long orderly lines. As sleek as bullets, their fur was tight to their bodies, their ears were back, and their heads were down.

After several weeks of living with the rats, Aargh was taken by how clever they were. Rats have a unique way of looking at the world, seeing many things that go completely unnoticed by most people. They find everything fascinating, and they never tire of exploring. Aargh learned many things concerning the greater workings of the world from the rats, along with several juicy stories for a later diary entry.

Unfortunately, being curious can lead to bad things, too. If rats got distracted by a scent or a sound, they might find themselves in a tight scrape or worse. This is where Aargh was able to help.

He taught the rats how to watch for behavioral patterns— like when the busboy emptied the trash or when a shop closed up for the night. He explained how to anticipate what a person might do instead of reacting when it was too late to avoid a confrontation. The rats eagerly listened to all of Aargh's stories and even began telling them to their pups. *The Parables of Wrudge & Aargh*, as they became known, have continued to be told for generations. A particular favorite has always been, *A House, an Orchid, and Roast Lamb: a mouthwatering tale of a magnificent home, a daring escape, and roast lamb.*

Touching Aargh on the arm, the little girl whispered, "There's a celebration happening on the street, and they're preparing to gather food."

You didn't have to be a rat to know a big celebration meant lots of food. Aargh's mouth watered at the thought. It had been quite some time since he'd eaten a meal fit for a wizard, and the idea of a celebration was appealing. The troubling thing was, he couldn't figure out what they were celebrating.

"The Day of Rain has long-since passed, the solstice was weeks ago, and Autumn Fall isn't for a while yet," he wondered aloud.

Thinking about the Fall of Autumn celebration made Aargh's stomach growl. There were always so many wonderful treats to sample! His favorites were the spiced pies, berry fritters, and hard cider with pickled apples.

"Mmm…We should find Wrudge and let him know that it's time to go," Aargh said, attempting to recognize the rats as they passed. It wasn't working out very well for him.

Pointing at their feet, the little girl replied lightheartedly, "I don't think we'll have to look far."

"Trusty Wrudge! You're always right where you need to be, aren't you?"

He certainly tried to be, and it made Wrudge happy knowing that Aargh noticed. Holding himself a little higher, off they went to find out what was happening above them on the streets of Gemini City.

By now, Aargh was quite familiar with the workings of the Underoof. They passed effortlessly through the tunnels; now left; now right; climbing up to the next level. In places where the tunnels opened to the street, they stayed away from the rays of light penetrating the darkness.

Aargh had become accustomed to the dimly lit, winding tunnels of the Underoof. The walls no longer closed in on him, and the floor didn't feel like it was moving under his feet. It felt good to overcome that feeling of helplessness he'd carried with him ever since the first day of classes. As they walked, Aargh even wondered if these tunnels might come in handy again someday.

Still, something bothered him as they climbed back into the alleyway. Then, Aargh realized what it was. Living in the darkness for so long, he'd forgotten how much his wizard's robes made him stand out in a crowd. For all they knew, the

Footman might still be looking for them, and he didn't want to take any chances. Everyone knew the Footman liked to post crude drawings of the wizards he was tracking on his office wall. He told people it was so he didn't forget to collect anyone, but the real reason was, he liked to use a heavy charcoal pencil to scratch them out after being hoisted.

"A disguise," Aargh thought, "not a problem for a wizard!"

Wizards have always fancied themselves masters of disguise, and Aargh was prepared. In the darkest corner of the alleyway, he turned his robes inside out. As breathtaking as they were on the outside, they were thoroughly plain on the inside. He did the same with his hat, which now flopped down like a hood. The only thing that gave Aargh a slight twinge was having to leave his feather behind. That had been a gift from the Lady of Sapphire Hall. She'd slipped it to him when the lord wasn't looking during the dessert course at the Sapphire Soirée. That was quite a night! The apple popover upside-down cake was particularly memorable.

As Aargh emerged, the little girl clapped in delight at his transformation. She liked to play dress-up, too and wondered if he liked tea.

Aargh was also pleased. Inspecting himself, he was confident that no one would recognize him dressed like this. No self-respecting wizard would allow themselves to be seen in public in such unassuming robes! Unfortunately, Aargh would be wrong about this and many other things before the day was over.

As they exited the alleyway, the bright sunlight blinded their eyes. Even through their shielding arms, they could see there was a celebration going on all along Middling Street. Vendors lined the street on both sides, confetti filled the air, and the music of drums and brass instruments reverberated off the buildings, booming from every direction. There was even a parade marching up Middling Street toward the Congregational House.

It was an imposing building with its smooth stone walls only interrupted by a grand staircase. Around midway up, a platform had been erected. It was lined with colorful buntings, and overhead, there were long banners billowing in the breeze. Along the sides, rows of heralding trumpets prepared their instruments, and, at intervals along the length of the stairs, the Honorable Palace Guarde stood at the ready (their name a holdover from an ancient time). The pièce de résistance was an ornate podium carefully placed right in the middle of the stage.

"It can't be. It simply can't be." Aargh said. "I need to get a closer look."

Carefully stepping between the revelers, carts, parade, and confetti, they picked their way along Upper Middling Street toward the Congregational House. That familiar tight feeling began to grip Aargh's heart once more, and he continued to talk to himself.

"I don't understand. The Master Prefect was elected only three years ago. He still has six years left to his term. Why would they have held an election already?"

Unbeknownst to Aargh, the previous Master Prefect had suddenly fallen ill and not been seen for several weeks. In his absence, the Upper Lords had elected a new Master Prefect, and that person was none other than the 15th Lord of Marble House! There he was, standing to the right of the podium, wearing the robes, the cowl, and the golden seal of the Master Prefect.

• • •

Looking out from the platform high above the street, the new Master Prefect surveyed his vast domain. He watched as ale flowed like water and children danced in the streets. Cheers rose and fell as the parade marched along. One by one, the Lower Lords bowed before him. Smugly, the Master Prefect nodded his head, all the while contemplating the powerful secrets he knew about each and every one of them.

He'd always wondered what it would be like to captain a ship, and now he would know. He'd be the one giving the orders from now on!

• • •

"What a terrible turn of events," Aargh said, trying to collect his thoughts. "Now, we'll never be safe in the city."

As horrified as Aargh was, what happened next would change his life forever. Far down Middling Street, a terrific blast of trumpets sounded, and a hush fell over the crowd. A massive steam-powered carriage began to laboriously roll north toward the Congregational House. Its gears churned, and steam billowed out of a tall, shiny smokestack. The parade stopped, and the revelers moved out of the way. Many stood on tiptoe and craned their necks, trying to see inside. Everyone was curious about the fantastic carriage.

"It must be someone important," a mother told her son.

"I've never seen a carriage like that before!" the boy said, excitedly standing on his tiptoes.

With a gasp of steam and grinding metal, the carriage settled at the foot of the stairs. To everyone's amazement and delight, it began to open, slowly transforming into a wondrous…well, no one knew what exactly! The center split open, and a man rose out of the middle wearing the most magnificent robes Aargh had ever seen. They were pure white with gold and silver embroidery glistening in the summer sun.

The new wizard surveyed the revelers, and they cowered under the weight of his stare.

"Who is this powerful wizard?" somebody asked.

"And why is he here?" another person whispered.

"What does he want?"

"Where did he come from?"

Then the wizard spoke with such intensity that the air vibrated, and the utensils on the tinker's cart rattled against one another.

"Master Prefect," he began, still facing the crowd. "On this auspicious day, we celebrate your investiture!"

The wizard raised his hands to the sky, and the crowd erupted with cheers–concern vanishing from their hearts.

He slowly lowered his arms and waited for the cheers to subside before continuing.

"I return to Gemini City and humbly come before you to offer my service. It would be my honor to serve as your advisor and as Wizard of the Council."

Once again, the crowd cheered. Everyone was jostling for a better look at the new wizard. They all wanted to see what was going to happen next.

"Master Prefect," the wizard said, turning to the stage, "Do you accept my offer?"

The revelers anxiously awaited his response, talking in hushed voices.

"What will the Master Prefect do?"

"I'm sure I don't know."

"He couldn't possibly turn the wizard down."

"This is so exciting!"

The Master Prefect gestured to his side, and the crowd went wild. The new Wizard of the Council moved toward the platform–his grand machine extending a walkway under his feet. Up and up, he moved until he was able to step right onto the stage. The wizard turned to the crowd, raised his hands, and Middling Street cheered again.

"Three cheers for the Master Prefect and his wizard! Huzzah! Huzzah! Huzzah!"

Aargh felt sick to his stomach. There hadn't been a council wizard in generations, and he'd never heard of a wizard who wore white robes before. There was something terribly wrong, but he couldn't put his finger on what it was. Aargh decided the best course of action was to get out of there, but the unthinkable happened as he started to leave. A flash of light caught Aargh's eye, and he looked up just in time to see the Wizard of the Council remove a long, smooth stick from within his dazzling white robes.

"A wand? What kind of a wizard would do such a thing?" Aargh reeled with a mixture of anguish and disgust.

Lifting the wand over his head, the wizard commanded, "Procella ignifera!"

At his command, the sky filled with fireworks, sizzling and crackling overhead. All up and down Middling Street, the people of Gemini City yelled with delight. With supreme hubris, the wizard stood there revealing magic to a world that didn't think it existed, and he was enjoying every moment.

"See! I told you there was real magic," a person near Aargh said.

"I know. We must not have had right wizards," an elderly lady agreed.

Aargh's head was spinning. What were these people talking about, and what had he just seen? Was it really magic? He needed time to think, and, more importantly, he needed to get his friends out of there before they were recognized.

Unfortunately, it was already too late for that. While Aargh had been busy trying to process everything that was happening, a slender man–dressed all in black and still as stone–stood quietly observing them from the shadows behind the Master Prefect.

• • •

Stifling a yawn, TTM stood high up the Congregational House's grand steps, thoroughly bored with the proceedings. He had little use for the gaudy pageantry of the ascension ceremony. He'd seen it all before, and he would see it all again. But then, something unusual *did* happen.

The wizard with the oversized robes, the little girl, and the dirty rat emerged from an alleyway, shielding their eyes against the bright sunlight. The trio then threaded their way through the celebration to get a better look at what was happening. He could see Aargh hanging on every word, and he noticed how Aargh tried to conceal his horror when the wizard produced a wand from within his robes. TTM saw everything, and he looked down on Gemini City with disgust.

"Look at them," TTM said scornfully. "Pitiful. They don't know anything. They go about their meaningless lives doing meaningless things."

TTM was appalled by how ill-informed everyone was—most notably the ridiculous lords and ladies who came to *his* house. It didn't matter how many people visited or how many Lords of Marble House there were; TTM would always remain the most intelligent person in the room.

"Right this way," he would say, installing visitors in the sitting room with a drink in one hand and ignorance in the other.

Whether they stood by the gaslit fireplace, sat in the reading nook, pondered the exquisite tapestries, or milled around near the buffet picking crayfish by the dozen off their icy bed, they never talked about anything of consequence. Even when the room was full of lords, no one ever said anything, and no one ever listened.

Early on, TTM had realized something interesting. Being that he had no standing in society, he was invisible. He could be inches away from someone, and they wouldn't even notice he was there. Such was the case with all of the help, and he used it to his advantage and amusement. Silently, he moved unseen through the cloud of cigar smoke and hot air as he tended to their so-called needs.

"A glass of brandy for you, sir? I do hope you enjoy it. It comes from our finest stock."

Although TTM never learned anything valuable (that information came from a far older and wiser source than these puffed-up buffoons), he did enjoy spending the evening correcting them in his mind. He never said anything out loud. He was too good at his job to make that mistake. Nobody would dare accuse him of anything less.

When he thought about it, which was quite often, he supposed this excellence was why he was still at Marble House. Most other people in his line of work lost their jobs when new lords moved in, but he'd remained. It never occurred to TTM that this was actually the result of everyone being terrified of him. Had he known, it would have pleased him greatly.

At times like these, TTM liked to pretend he was a renowned professor at the Gemini City School of Wizarding. In fact, that was what he was doing right now during the ascension of the latest Lord of Marble House to Master Prefect. With his head held high, TTM imagined talking down to the lowly students. It wouldn't matter if they listened or not; they would never know as much as he did.

Bored with the cheering and bowing and drinking (can't forget the drinking as there was a lot of that going on), TTM slipped away in his mind…

"Ahem," he began, making sure to get everyone's attention. "We are here, on the steps of the Congregational House, to explore the history of what was once known as the Quadropolis. Of the four cities, only the two southern districts still exist today, now known as Gemini City.

"The Congregational House, originally named Middle Building, was erected in the exact center of the Quadropolis with four long roads stretching out to the north, south, east, and west. Only the southern road remains, now referred to as Middling Street. The east and west roads became the Once-Great Wall, and Middle Building Street North is now known as Old Middle-Forest Road. This ancient pass is the focus of our lecture, today…"

TTM went on this way for quite some time, dryly relating the burning of Eastie and Westie Nort–the towns that, long ago, were located beyond the Once-Great Wall. Needless to say, his lecture was from the Sowtown's perspective. The Norters didn't see it the same way, but their story had been lost to history.

While he waxed on to his imaginary students about the fall of the northern cities, the heralds began to prepare their trumpets. Proud and tall, the trumpeters raised their long horns, adorned with banners bearing the emblem of the city or the Master Prefect's seal.

"…gone–wiped from the face of the earth. And since there wasn't a single tree left standing, not even a wizard could have told anyone what had happened; although, people still thought it had something to do with magic.

"It's a complete mystery where the people of Eastie and Westie Nort disappeared to, but I'm sure you've all heard the folktales and the old nursery rhyme:

> *One pickup penny, lying in the wood.*
> *Two dark wizards, facing as they stood.*
> *Three was their number, magic cast in blood.*
> *Put the penny back, or the city's gone for good."*

As the heralds waited for the right moment to signal the Master Prefect's exit, the sun glinted off their ornately etched bells. TTM nearly jumped out of his skin when they started to play, ripped from his reverie and back into the gaudy display of pomp and circumstance. Of course, *jumping out of his skin* only meant that his left pinky finger twitched a tiny bit to the right, but he would still have to tell *BoB* about it. His displeasure didn't last long, though. As he looked over the shoulder of the Master Prefect, past the new Wizard of the Council, down the elegant stone steps, and out over the celebrating city, TTM saw the little wizard trying to make his ill-fated escape.

"What fun," TTM mumbled under his breath. "And there's the Footman, too. A game of cat and mouse! I wonder who will win?"

TTM watched as the mice bobbed and weaved through the revelers. They were trying to move quickly but without drawing attention to themselves. First, they paused; then they skittered to the left; then to the right.

"Oh, look out!"

TTM watched as the trio almost got hit by *Glenda's The Gilded Gooseberry Cart.* It was a narrow escape. Then, they scurried under the farm stand umbrellas and made their way through the parade to get to the other side of the road.

The cat, for his part, was moving in for the kill.

For a brief moment, Aargh felt the cool freedom of the darkened alleyway, but as they were about to step into the shadows, the Footman barred their way. Aargh froze with fear as he stared down at them.

"Run! We must run!" was all Aargh could think.

Then, with surprising speed, the cat pounced!

As TTM watched from high up the Congregational House's steps, something unexpected happened. When the Footman reached out for the wizard, he appeared to freeze. If

TTM wasn't mistaken, it even looked like the Footman was hovering in the air with both feet off the ground. He had launched himself at his quarry and then froze, right there, in the middle of Middling Street! TTM couldn't believe his eyes, but he knew what it meant. Magic. Powerful magic.

TTM stealthily took a step back into the shadows. "Soon," he hissed. "My moment will come."

The Footman, on the other hand, wasn't having as much fun. He fell with a crash but not on top of the wizard or the girl. Where had they gone? Twice, they'd vanished from right in front of him. Was he losing his touch?

It was all too much to process, so he decided there was nothing for it; he would go see Buss and drink some carriage fuel. Actually, he would drink a lot of it and hope that he forgot all about the wizard, the girl, and was that a rat following them?

"Maybe it's time for a holiday."

Chapter 5

MAGIC IS REAL

Completely lost in his thoughts, Aargh sat pensively in the clearing. He was trying to piece together all that had happened. Usually, coming to his special place was calming, but today, no matter how hard he tried, he couldn't come up with any answers. There were only questions, and those questions kept rising the way a river threatens to overflow its banks after a storm.

"It's a revelation…no, a miracle, really. I've devoted my entire life to studying magic, and in an instant, I find out it was all for nothing. How did the Wizard of the Council discover magic? Where did he get that despicable wand? And how does she have magic, too? She's so young. What am I missing?"

As crucial as figuring out who and what the new wizard was, Aargh's thoughts kept returning to the child. He'd never met anyone like her before. She was so innocent and fragile but in other ways strong, even powerful. How could she be both at the same time? And although she was many things, there was no question that the thing he loved most about her was her kindness.

Aargh searched his feelings and realized he was growing fond of her. The bundle of robes he'd met on the street that day seemed to give him purpose. A different kind of purpose. The kind of purpose that made him feel like everything else was becoming less important.

Aargh watched as she scratched Wrudge's belly. She was giggling as he rolled this way and that so she could reach his best scratch places. One leg up. Flat on his back. Twisted to the left. Wrudge was milking it!

"Wrudge never lets *me* scratch his belly like that," Aargh laughed to himself.

The more Aargh thought about it, the more he realized the little girl inspired (or maybe taught?) him to think and do things he'd never considered before. Clearly, Wrudge felt the same way. However, he obviously had many lessons yet to learn because no matter how hard he tried, Aargh still couldn't understand all that was happening.

"How could I have missed it? Surely at some point in my life, I must have seen magic before, even if it was something small. Maybe a coincidence or a surprise?"

There was an uneasy feeling growing in his belly. It wasn't only that he'd missed it; it was that he should have noticed. He was Historian and Keeper of the General Generations, after all. It was his job to notice things and record them.

Then, Aargh had the glimmer of an idea. It was far away, like the tiny point of light at the end of a long tunnel. He seized on the thought and focused with all of his might. Then it became clear.

"Maybe that's it? Maybe I need to think back to when I was a boy?"

Aargh thought about how children view everything that happens in the world as magical. He was all too aware that as people aged, they often became jaded and cautious, always expecting a rational explanation, or underlying motive, for everything. But children didn't view the world that way.

Unfortunately, this revelation didn't make Aargh feel better because he couldn't remember his childhood. Not a single thing. Although he often tried to think back to his life before wizarding school, his memories seemed to begin when he made the first entry in his diary.

All through wizarding school, the boys wondered and joked about being able to cast spells. They'd play tricks on each other, trying to make their friends and teachers believe something magical had happened.

There was the time Garthelwaite hovered over his bed suspended by fishing line. That resulted in several boys getting to peel potatoes in the kitchen with old Fussybudget. They never pulled that stunt again; of that, you can be sure!

Or the time Bartlebee made it look like everyone's familiars had turned into toads. Well, everyone's but young Fizzbain's since his familiar *was* a toad. That had the class in an uproar for a week and poor Bartlebee sleeping in the stalls. It had been worth it, though, he'd told Aargh, getting to see the look on Professor Snoodlebood's face as he tried to explain what had happened.

The professors were never really fooled, though. They would always say the same thing, "Wizards have been talking to trees for centuries. Don't you think they would have noticed if there was other magic in the world?" and that would quickly put an end to the discussion.

"They were entirely wrong," Aargh said to himself, thinking back to his days at wizarding school. "Completely and utterly wrong."

Today had proven that. He'd seen the Wizard of the Council perform magic with his own eyes, and twice now, Aargh had escaped the Footman in a way that could only be explained by the use of magic.

Aargh carefully examined everything that had happened. As the Footman loomed over them, the only thing he could think of was to run as fast as he could. This was a ridiculous thought for a refined wizard, but it was what he thought, nevertheless. Therefore, if he hadn't done anything, it had to have been the little girl. Somehow she'd cast a spell to slow time or make them move very fast. It had to be!

"It all happened so quickly," Aargh said, trying to remember every detail. But he couldn't even recall the path they'd taken. One moment, he was sure they were going to be strung up by their feet, and the next, they were safely in the hole in the wall telling the rats all about their narrow escape from the Footman. That brought Aargh right back to where he'd begun: magic is unquestionably real.

This thought weighed heavily on his mind. It seemed impossible that someone with no training could perform such impressive feats of magic.

Magic.

Aargh realized that he'd come to fully embrace the idea—even if he didn't understand it—and if there was magic in the world, he had to learn more about it.

What Aargh didn't know was that any father could have explained children's magic to him. There's nothing more cherished, more special, or holds more power over someone than the spell a daughter casts over her father. It's some of the most potent magic in the world, but Aargh, the novice, was only on *Lesson One: So, you're a parent? Your child is now the center of your universe.*

As Aargh watched her, a thought began to bubble up in his mind.

"Maybe she can teach me?" he mused.

That was how Aargh learned: *Lesson Two: Your children teach you more than you teach them.*

Aargh looked around the clearing and decided to let Wrudge and the little girl keep playing. Then, he slipped off the log and laid back on the soft green grass. The trees' tops framed the pale blue sky, and he dreamily watched the clouds as they floated high above them.

"Hey, that one kind of looks like a garble," he said, stretching his arms above his head and yawning.

It wasn't long before the bundle of giggles came over and snuggled up next to him, for who doesn't love a nap on a warm summer day? But naps are accompanied by dreams, and dreams make sure you never forget.

"Run! Run!" Aargh could hear himself calling out as the trio raced toward safety. The world was a blur, and all Aargh could think was, "We have to run!"

In the blink of an eye, they'd rushed past the Footman, hurtled down the alleyway, and disappeared into the tunnels.

Word of their return sped through the Underoof, and it wasn't long before rats were jostling at the entrance of their hole to hear what had happened. They hung on every word as Aargh told them of the Lord of Marble House's ascension to the position of Master Prefect and, most importantly, his acceptance of the white-robed wizard's offer.

The rats had stories, too. Thanks to Aargh and his teachings, they'd been able to move unseen through the revelry, collecting more than enough food to fill their stores. They thanked him many times, but Aargh's mind was distant and troubled. He asked the rats if they knew a secret way to the forest, and naturally, they did. As he'd previously observed, the tunnels ran everywhere in the city, even north, beyond the wall.

Through it all, a vague darkness continued to plague Aargh's mind. He tried to fight it back, but he couldn't stop it from creeping in from all sides. He didn't want to! He couldn't be a wizard anymore! He didn't know how to do real magic!

Aargh woke suddenly. They weren't in the tunnels. They'd escaped to the safety of his secret clearing in the forest. It was a place he'd visited often over the years. Aargh wasn't sure why, but being here felt comforting, like coming home.

Throughout the forest, there were ancient paths. They were overgrown now, but Aargh could still see them. He knew they were once part of a city north of the wall, but he didn't know much else about it—only rumors and children's stories. He often asked the forest trees about them, but they were too young to be much help. Being that he was a Spire Historian, Aargh could tell you anything you wanted to about Gemini City, but since he spent most of his time talking to young Sowtownie trees, he didn't have much knowledge of the distant past.

Aargh noticed that Wrudge had come back from foraging and was sound asleep, tucked into the little girl's arm.

"What a spoiled rat!" Aargh chuckled as he stretched and got up to build a fire.

Although Aargh would never hurt a living tree, he was far from the city's gas, oil, and coal. He knew they needed fire for warmth, to cook dinner, and to keep the flies at bay. Aargh often talked with the trees and knew they didn't mind as long as he was careful and only burned fallen wood. The trees trusted Aargh, and he trusted the trees.

Over the years, Aargh had often wondered why more people didn't visit the forest. The Once-Great Wall had long since crumbled to ruin in places, and it wasn't difficult to cross into the northern woods. Maybe it was that people had become accustomed to the city's noisy bustle or that they were uncomfortable being surrounded by the gentle buzz of the bugs and birdsong? Aargh thought it was soothing.

As he sat there contemplating, Aargh poked at the fire's hot embers. It almost looked as though red and orange worms were crawling around the pieces of charred wood. As he watched them wriggle, his thoughts kept coming back to recent events. He came to the conclusion that he'd have to get used to brown.

"No more fine robes or kingly dinners for you, Aarghath-lain. I guess it's time to hang up your wizarding hat."

As Aargh saw it, two paths lay before him. He could go back and figure out what was going on or go forward and protect the child. Or, more accurately, he would *have* to go back and figure out what was going on, but for now, he would go forward and make sure the child was safe. She was his responsibility now, and with wizarding behind him, it looked like a new adventure was taking shape in his mind.

Aargh had never known happiness greater than those weeks spent living in the forest; at least, not that he could remember. It felt safe, like the troubles of the world were far away. He knew this wasn't true, but he tried hard not to think about it too much.

They passed the time playing hide and seek, discovering monsters in the clouds, splashing each other in the cold streams that ran down from the mountains, and building fairy houses out of pine needles and bark. On warm summer afternoons, they snoozed under the shady trees. In the cool evenings, they sat close together, roasting strawberries and apples over the open fire. When it was time to go to bed, they would lay back and count the stars. But through it all, the darkness still played at the edges of his mind. Aargh knew that all he had to do was ask, but he didn't want to.

"No! I don't want to!" Aargh called out.

"It's okay. You don't have to, if you don't want to," a soothing voice gently reassured him.

Aargh hadn't realized that he'd nodded off, but as he shook off the last vestiges of sleep, he turned to the child and said, "Unfortunately, I do."

So, Aargh gathered himself (and his robes) and set off into the woods. Soon, he came upon a tall, old pine tree. He settled down on the soft bed of needles that spread out from the trunk and spoke to the tree. At first, it was mostly polite conversation. In other words, Aargh sat quietly while the tree shared many stories, but his mind soon began to follow its roots to the future. It was second nature, and he simply had to know what the new wizard's purpose was.

"That's funny," Aargh thought quizzically. "That root ended rather abruptly. No matter. I'll try another," but that root ended, too, and another root, and another. Now he was speaking to a different tree.

Nothing.

Alarmed, Aargh asked himself, "What's going on?"

Tree after tree and root after root, he searched, but no matter what branch of knowledge he followed, he couldn't see the future. He couldn't see the future!

"Oh no!" he called out. "We have to get back!"

• • •

Still and silent, the Congregational House waited as rain pattered on the glass of the elaborate dome. Even on days when the sky was sullen, the Grand Rotunda was magnificent. High above, the Capam Speculo sat on top of the building like a window into the heavens–an architectural marvel that no modern-day craftsman had been able to equal. The truth was, no architect had even tried.

The Wizard of the Council traced the rain as it traveled down the interlocking glass triangles toward the roof. Once it reached the bottom, it ran along the long beveled glass ceiling of the hallway toward Middling Street. The light of the oil lamps reflected and shimmered under the flowing water, illuminating the hallway the way sunlight looks when it peeks through the leaves of a tree.

"Trees," the Wizard of the Council hissed to himself, "Who made them the keepers of the world's knowledge?"

"What was that?" the Master Prefect asked.

"Nothing, my Lord. I was wondering if you had considered extending your influence overseas."

"I believe we should focus on Gemini City first. The rest will come."

"Yes. You are very wise," the Wizard of the Council capitulated. "Might I raise an issue that may be of slight concern?"

The Master Prefect nodded, and the wizard continued.

"It has come to my attention that a few of the Upper Lords had a meeting recently."

"That's not unusual," the Master Prefect dismissed. "It's part of their job to discuss things."

"It's more about what they were discussing."

"I'm listening."

"They are, how shall I say, *uneasy* with the fact that you're making policy changes without consulting them first. The Upper Lords are interested in having some form of oversight. Maybe a committee to review your decisions? Most notably, where the workings of the city are concerned."

"What?" the Master Prefect exclaimed, his voice echoing around the rotunda and down the long hallway. Rising from his chair, which looked more like a throne than a chair, he began to pace.

"So, they aren't happy with the way I'm running things? I bet it's that sniveling Lord of Quartz Hall. That house is barely on Upper Middling Street. Not even sure he should be a lord. You are right. I might need to deal with that. Let's see; there was that matter of a rather large wager last year... anyway, he's always whining about everything in that irritating high-pitched voice of his. Maybe it's time for me to give a little demonstration to show them all who holds the real power in this city."

The wizard smiled a crooked smile.

The Master Prefect continued, "It must be something that can't be ignored. Something *elemental*."

And with that, the Wizard of the Council stopped smiling and started paying much closer attention. What exactly did the Master Prefect mean by *elemental?*

The Master Prefect continued in a commanding tone, "I want you to create a lightning storm. Not just any storm, either. I want the skies darkened to the horizon and lightning to strike at your command. I want them to squirm."

Surprised by the magnitude of the request, the wizard began to respond, "A fine idea, indeed, but that would require a substantial amount of magic to produce."

"Oh, so there *are* limits to your power," the Master Prefect retorted wryly.

"I didn't say I couldn't do it. I was explaining that magic of that nature requires a special kind of power."

"And you're saying that your fancy wand doesn't have that kind of power?"

"Not at all, but I would require a familiar to channel it."

"Then get one," the Master Prefect said offhandedly as if familiars were a dime a dozen.

The Wizard of the Council gritted his teeth indignantly. What the Master Prefect didn't know about magic could fill a spellbook!

Regaining his composure, the wizard said, a little too politely, "And where do you propose I find such a familiar? Have you come across any during your trips *downtown?*"

The wizard knew he was treading on dangerous terrain but also knew that he held all the cards.

A dark flash of anger passed across the Master Prefect's face, but before he could respond, a slender man slipped out of the shadows and addressed the two men.

"I believe I might be of service," came TTM's slow drawl.

Both men started at the sound and did their best to avert their eyes.

"I didn't realize you were still here," the Master Prefect said, addressing the third pillar to the left but one. It was tall, black, slender, and cold–not unlike TTM.

Taking no notice, TTM continued. He spared no detail as he recounted events from Aargh's arrival at Marble House through the hovering Footman. After many years of practice speaking to his imaginary students, TTM was confident that he knew how to spin a yarn, and it was true. He quickly had both men wrapped around his finger. It felt good to have a captive audience.

The Master Prefect, for his part, was seething with anger, ready to string up that little wizard by his toes the first chance he got. He hadn't forgotten the loss of his prized Golden Orchid, and he was looking for revenge. What the Master Prefect didn't know was that the Footman was lying prostrate under a table at Blunder-Buss' Underground Ale House, having consumed enough carriage fuel to power the wizard's metal contraption for a week. It was unlikely that he would be getting himself off the floor, let alone stringing anyone up, for quite some time.

The wizard, on the other hand, was far away, deep in thought. How had he not known about the little girl? Even now, when he tried to remember her from the crowd, she seemed distant. Misty. Magical.

The more he thought about her, the more pleased he became. Who cared if he hadn't noticed her? He knew about her now, and that was all that mattered. With a familiar containing that much power, he could move mountains, and the best part was he wouldn't need the pompous Master Prefect anymore.

"I'll create a light show the likes of which no one has ever seen before. Then, I'll dispense with the Master Prefect and all of the other lords once and for all. Maybe Marble House, too, for good measure," the wizard reflected. "A little girl. What could be easier? Soon, it will all be mine. All of it."

Chapter 6

THE HERMIT OF THE WOOD

Impossible! Aargh's mind was racing. Not being able to see the future had really shaken him. Is the future hidden? Is it not there? What could possibly make it disappear? The thought of a world without a future was too much to process.

What Aargh didn't know was this wasn't the first time the future had gone dark. If any trees had survived from ancient times, they could have told him why, but the northern forest was too young to remember the last time this had happened.

As Aargh watched the little girl playing hide and seek with Wrudge–which mostly meant she ran around while Wrudge pointed here and there–he was sad. Aargh didn't want to take her away from this, but he knew they couldn't stay. The only thing he was sure of was that he needed to find out what was going on.

Aargh's thoughts shifted to the day when he'd watched the new wizard produce a wand from within his white robes. Even now, as his world was beginning to awaken, he couldn't understand the wand, and more questions played across his mind.

Where had he gotten it? Did the wizard do something to make it magical? Maybe his eyes had deceived him? No, it was a wand, of that he was sure. The more Aargh thought about it, the more determined he became. Wand or no wand, he had to return to Gemini City.

"We know," a soft voice answered.

Snapping back into the moment, Aargh saw that his companions had stopped playing and were standing right in front of him.

"The wizard is like that mean man in the street, isn't he?" she asked. "He's forgotten his lessons."

Aargh found it hard to answer the child. He didn't want her to know about such things. Looking at her standing there, he wished she could keep playing in the summer sun as if the rest of the world didn't even exist. But, somewhere inside, he knew the world's troubles wouldn't stay hidden for long, so he decided to be honest with her.

"Yes, Little One, the wizard has forgotten his lessons. I don't know what he wants or what he'll do, but something is wrong. I need to go back and find out. I'm afraid that if I don't, something terrible will happen. I don't know why. I just feel it."

"So do I," she said, taking his hand. "Wrudge feels it, too."

With three heavy hearts, they set off back along the path that had brought them here in the first place. Aargh tried to lighten the mood by naming all of the trees they passed, but it was no use. They were all too worried.

The last time the trio had hidden from the world, they'd returned to find a huge celebration, a new Master Prefect, and the arrival of the wizard. It was impossible to guess what they would find this time. None of them thought it would be anything good.

"That's strange," Aargh said, removing his hat and scratching his head. "How did we get here? That's Ransom Ravine."

Aargh knew Ransom Ravine ran along the northeastern edge of the forest. The foothills of Mount Ardilakk rose dramatically from its far bank. The ravine had earned its name long ago when the Marauders had used it as a hideout. People still believed riches beyond their wildest imagination were hidden at the bottom of the gorge, but the way in was a secret. The outlaws had guarded that critical piece of information so well that it was lost when the Palace Guarde drove them from the forest.

"We must have taken a wrong turn," Aargh said, not feeling terribly confident with his assessment of the situation.

They appeared to be moving in the opposite direction from where they wanted to go. He'd never gotten *this* lost before.

Turning around, they tried again, retracing their steps and moving south. Around midday, they stumbled upon Falling Rock, and Aargh knew something was wrong. There was no way he was this turned around. Once again, they were moving north instead of south. If he was this topsy-turvy, something else was at play.

Aargh decided they should stop for lunch so he could have a chance to think. Everyone thought that was a splendid idea, though it wasn't necessarily *thinking* they wanted to do. All three had grown tired of walking in circles, and the berries they'd been gathering along the way were calling to them. There was nothing like taking a walk in the forest during the summer. Everywhere you looked, there was something beautiful to brighten your day or, even better, something to fill your hungry belly.

As Aargh tried to make sense of their misdirection, he absentmindedly rolled a berry around between his fingers. No matter how hard he tried, he wasn't able to figure out what was happening. He obviously couldn't avoid it, and he couldn't see what it was, so why not play along for a while?

"Well," he said, standing up, "there's nothing for it. We'll have to see where the road leads us. For better or worse, at least we'll get some answers."

"You might want to wash your hand first," a giggling little voice suggested.

Aargh looked down and saw that he'd squished the berry he was holding. His hand was dyed a deep purplish blue. Aargh didn't know why but that tickled him, and he started to laugh. Wrudge, with both forefeet clamped over his mouth, couldn't hold it in any longer. He let out a piercing, high-pitched squeak, and that, as they say, was that! All three burst into a fit of laughter–a doubled over, holding-their-stomachs kind of laugher (except for Wrudge, who was literally rolling around on the grass).

The stress of returning to the city–and not knowing what they would find when they got there–had been building up within them throughout the day. All that stress had to come out one way or another, and laughing was the best way any of them could think of at the moment.

After they calmed down, and with much lighter hearts, they set off again. This time, Aargh didn't even try to find their way back to the city. Instead, whenever they came to a crossroads, they simply kept walking. Whatever direction their feet took them was the direction they went. Before long, Aargh saw something entirely unfamiliar that intrigued him.

In a particularly dense part of the wood, the trees parted to form an open space. It was a perfect circle, ringed by tall, pencil-like trees with broad canopies spreading high above their heads. As they entered the clearing, the sounds of the forest grew softer, almost muffled.

They could see that within the outer circle, there were two inner circles. The first was made of smooth, flat stones that had been carefully placed on a bed of bright white chalk. Wrudge stopped to investigate.

The next ring was a shallow stream that didn't appear to have a beginning or an end, infinitely flowing counter to what was wise. The sunlight glistened off the sparkling creek, and the second of their party stopped to dip her hot, tired feet in the cool water.

Aargh, the last of their party, continued on. He was fascinated by the center of the clearing where a hut had been fashioned from living trees. The closer he got to it, the less he perceived the world around him. All of his thoughts were focused on the hut.

It wouldn't have been surprising at all if someone had mistaken the trees for giants, hunched over with their hands on each other's shoulders and their heads together. Aargh had never seen anything like it. He half-expected the Arbor team captain to yell, "Break!" as if they were huddling together before the next big play on the Mundsling Field.

As Aargh dreamily moved closer, one thought kept wafting through his foggy mind: This must be the dwelling of a powerful wizard, a wizard who had mastered the mysteries of the world. He wanted to be scared. Really, he did. He even tried to tell himself that he needed to be afraid of this mysterious cottage carefully hidden in the woods, but he couldn't. It was too compelling. It was definitely magical, and he had to know more.

"Then what are you waiting for, young Aargh? Come in! Please, come in!" a familiar voice beckoned as a tall wizard, dressed in purple and gold embroidered robes, emerged from the hut.

"Aldenthwaine," Aargh gasped, and with an enormous sense of relief, he rushed over to greet his long-lost mentor.

"Whoa. Not so fast. Let me look at you. It's been a while, hasn't it?"

The wizard studied Aargh from head to toe and said, "Your disguise doesn't fool me. I see that you have splendid robes, indeed. But you have traveled far and must be tired. Come in. I'll make you some nice lavender tea, and we can talk for a while."

Mesmerized by the sight of his mentor, and without so much as a glance back at his companions, Aargh disappeared into the shadowy hut.

• • •

Wrudge sniffed the chalk cautiously and touched the surface of the smooth stones. Slowly and carefully, he made his way around the circle. There was only more of the same. It wasn't long before he realized that going 'round and 'round wasn't getting him anywhere. Although rats are easily distracted, they also don't spend much time on any single thought, so although the ring of chalk was intriguing, it was time to move on.

Snapping out of it, Wrudge tried to cross into the inner circle but couldn't. At first, he felt a slight tug at his insides, but as he moved over the stones, he began to feel so heavy that he had to plop down on the dusty ground. Luckily, being a rat, Wrudge's first thought was: don't panic. It wasn't the first time he'd gotten stuck, and it wouldn't be the last. Rats are masters of squeezing into tight spaces. Obviously, that means they get stuck now and then, but every rat knows that if they panicked, well, let's just say that wouldn't result in anything good.

Although many people think of rats as simple-minded, rats prefer to think of themselves as practical. Therefore, Wrudge's first thought was, "If I can't go forward, maybe I should go backward?"

That worked nicely, and in a moment, Wrudge was back on the outside, looking in.

Another stalwart quality of rats is persistence. If a rat wants something or needs something for the colony, they're going to get it! Therefore, Wrudge tried again. No luck. Again and again, he tried to cross the circle, but every time he was pulled to the ground before reaching the other side.

That was when he looked up and saw his girl crying. She was also trying to get to Aargh, but she couldn't get past the stream. Every time she tried to step over it, she slipped backwards onto the grass with a thump. Soon she was frantically racing around the circle. Wrudge tried to keep up, but his ring was much larger, and she ran ahead of him. Suddenly, there was a scream!

As Wrudge rounded the bend, he could see behind the hut. His girl had collapsed onto the ground. No matter how hard he tried, Wrudge couldn't get to her.

• • •

"But why didn't you tell anyone?" Aargh asked, unable to comprehend why Aldenthwaine had hidden his discovery.

"Because it was too dangerous. Don't you see? Can you imagine what this power could do in the wrong hands? At first, I felt as you do, excited about my discovery. I couldn't wait to share it with all of the other wizards. It was the greatest discovery since the founding of our guild! I wrote down everything I learned, and I called it the *One True Book of Spells*. It was to be my crowning achievement—my magnum opus! But with every new page, I became more and more worried about it falling into the wrong hands. In the end, I retreated to my hut, far away from prying eyes. I couldn't let the evil of the world exploit what I had discovered."

"But it could also do so much good! How could revealing it be such a bad thing?" Aargh insisted.

"Ah, yes. Ever the optimist. Young Aargh, I am much older and, perhaps, wiser than you. There exist evils in the world that you couldn't imagine, even if you tried. No, there was only one path for me: hiding. But that didn't mean I had to be alone. I needed to find someone I could trust with this knowledge. Someone who would be willing to do anything to keep it from falling into the wrong hands. That is why—"

At that moment, a scream pierced Aargh's mind, and he regained control of his thoughts. "Oh no!" he blurted out. "She's hurt."

Aargh rushed out of the hut, shielding his eyes and squinting in the bright sunlight.

"Where are you, Little One?" he called as he moved around the innermost circle.

She was lying on the ground, holding her leg. She looked fuzzy and out of focus. Aargh shook his head absently as he stepped over the stream, and his eyes cleared.

He kneeled down beside the child and said, "There, there. Let me see it."

"No," she recoiled, "It hurts."

"I won't touch it, I promise, but I need to take a look. Did you twist your ankle? It doesn't look so bad. I think you were more shocked than hurt. Don't you think so?"

Now that she knew it wasn't so bad, she relaxed a little (as not being *so bad* has always been, and always will be, an important thing for children).

"Yes. I tripped on that funny-looking rock over there. The one that's sticking out of the ground."

Aargh followed her finger to where she was pointing and saw a flat stone partially covered by moss. The way it barely stuck out above the tufts of grass troubled him. If he hadn't known better, he might have thought it was intentionally placed there to trip someone.

"Are you feeling any better? I think maybe I should check out that rock."

She nodded, and he moved to take a better look at what had tripped her.

Wrudge could see Aargh and his little girl, but he couldn't get their attention. He watched intently as Aargh moved toward the stone, but it wasn't the only one planted in the shade behind the hut.

As Aargh passed the first headstone, he read the inscription aloud.

Asmodeus, the snake.
Stealthy observer of the world
and most remarkable familiar.
Your presence will be missed.

The closer Aargh got to the mossy stone, the more worried he felt. He was finally becoming scared, terrified actually, but he had to see what was on that stone. He could feel it pulling him closer. There was something terrible waiting for him under that green carpet of moss, of that, he was sure.

Aargh bent down and slowly reached out to roll back the moss. It felt cool and soft under his fingers. Aargh's blood turned to ice in his veins as he read the words etched onto the surface of the stone.

Here lies Aldenthwaine.
Former Wizard of the Spire and
writer of the One True Book of Spells.

He'd been tricked! Aargh tried to turn around, but he found it hard to move. Wrudge watched as Aargh drifted off the ground. He looked as if he was attempting to swim through the air—his robes floating all around him.

The illusion obscuring the true nature of the clearing faded. They could see the old, abandoned hut, the dry stream, and the overgrown ring of stones. In the middle of it all stood the Wizard of the Council. Aargh screamed, but it was the distant, muffled sound of someone underwater.

Wrudge ran as fast as he could.

Looking back over his shoulder, he saw the anguished look on Aargh's face as the Wizard of the Council grabbed his girl and disappeared into the forest. At that moment, the spell seemed to break, and Aargh fell to the ground. He was up in an instant, running into the trees after them.

Wrudge ran faster. There was no time to lose!

Chapter 7

NO MATTER WHICH ROAD YOU TAKE, THEY ALL LEAD HOME

Somewhere ahead in the distance, Aargh heard the faint snap of a twig. Doubled over and trying to catch his breath, he stood there gasping.

"It's no use. There's no way. I can't catch them. The brush is too thick," Aargh explained to himself.

He'd been forcing his way through the forest undergrowth for the better part of an hour, but the branches and brambles wouldn't let him through.

"I'm your friend," Aargh pleaded with the woods. "Let me pass! Please, let me pass!" but it was no use. The plants only tugged at his robes even harder.

The Wizard of the Council, on the other hand, seemed to move with uncanny ease through the grasping limbs and prickly briars.

Aargh tried to hold on to the notion that he could catch them, but all too soon, the wizard had become only flashes of white between the tree trunks. Then there was only the distant sound of things breaking underfoot, and finally, the faint whoosh of leafy branches snapping back into place. That was when reality had set in. The wizard had taken his precious Little One, and they were gone.

Aargh looked down to ask Wrudge what to do, but he was gone, too. It wasn't unusual for Wrudge to slip away, most often for a quick snack, but this was different. Worried that Wrudge might still be stuck at the hut, Aargh decided to turn back and search for him.

It was difficult, stepping into those circles again. This time, there was no tug at his body or muffling of his ears. It was just dead, and although Aldenthwaine had disappeared from the wizarding school years ago, Aargh had always hoped to see him again.

Aargh often daydreamed that Aldenthwaine was off on some grand adventure. Maybe he'd found a way to cross Mount Ardilakk? That would have been something. Or possibly, he'd discovered what happened to the ancient city that once stood under the feet of the northern forest. Anything seemed possible to Aargh except the one thing that had actually happened–Aldenthwaine had discovered magic.

"You would never know it, looking at this," Aargh said to himself.

The clearing appeared to have been abandoned for many years. The ring of stones was so overgrown that he had to part the tall grass to pass through it–sending a cloud of tiny flies into the air.

Aargh walked around the circle, but he never stopped looking at the hut. Now a shell of rotting wood, it must have been magnificent. What a beautiful place to spend your days, literally surrounded by trees. He hadn't forgotten about Wrudge, but there was no sign of him either, which was a bit of a relief.

"He must be okay," Aargh consoled himself feebly but knowing in his heart that things were not going well for any of them.

It had been so long since Aargh was truly alone that he wasn't sure how to process his feelings. He hadn't realized how accustomed he'd become to hearing that little voice. And how could he possibly hope to face the Wizard of the Council without Wrudge by his side?

A strange feeling began to overtake him. Aargh wondered if he'd never fully realized how much he relied on Wrudge? Oh, Aargh always told people how much they were a team; that much was true. And, he was the first (and only) person to defend Wrudge when unpleasant things were said. But had he given their partnership a second thought? They just were, as far as Aargh was concerned, and that was enough, right?

Aargh began to second guess how he treated Wrudge. And worse, he began to worry that he might have taken his faithful companion's presence for granted. He did brush him twice a day. That was good. And he treated him with respect; there was no doubt about that. There was also no question that Aargh knew how important it was for a wizard to have a strong bond with his familiar, but still, something nagged at the back of his mind—something vague and intangible, murky and foreboding.

Hunched over, weighed down by despair, Aargh knew he couldn't simply stand there feeling sorry for himself. That wasn't helpful to anyone. He needed to keep moving, but each step strained every muscle in his body. He felt such pain at the loss of Aldenthwaine, Wrudge, and the little girl. It was almost as if part of him had been torn away, leaving him raw and exposed. He knew he couldn't stop now, but how could he go on this way? He could barely move.

Aargh reached up to wipe the sweat from his brow and froze. His hand was still stained from when he'd squished the berry, and the sight of it stunned him. Images of his friends playing in the woods flashed through his mind. It was precisely the push he needed to overcome the oppressiveness of his thoughts and take action.

In an effort to get himself back on track, Aargh began talking to himself. He slapped his knees, stood up straight, and said, "There's nothing for it! I can't follow through the brush, which means I'll have to stick to the old paths. What do you think?"

"I think that's a great idea," Aargh replied.

"Good! I'm glad we agree."

"Do you have any idea where we are?"

"Not a wit."

"Me neither, but that's never stopped us before!"

This was undoubtedly true. It wasn't the first time Aargh had been lost in the forest, and (if he had anything to say about it) it wouldn't be the last. He knew the trick was to keep a cool head, get your bearings, and move with purpose. These were all things he could do.

"Let's see," Aargh said, with an elbow in one hand and the other hand on his chin. "Where am I?"

The forest was enormous, and although Aargh knew it well, no one ever knows a forest *that* well. If you were to take a few steps off in a new direction, you could find yourself completely lost.

"Step one," Aargh said with a confident air, "I must determine which direction is south."

This step was easy because even though the trees grew tall, and Aargh did not, Mount Ardilakk stood high above everything. It towered over the forest, and the city, like a massive arrow pointing due north. And judging by its location, Aargh was far off the beaten track or, at the very least, *his* beaten track. He knew this part of the wood was called Westiewood and that few people traveled this way because it ended abruptly at the foot of a tall wall of stone. That side of the valley looked like the earth had cracked and dropped a hundred feet straight down. There was even a Westiewood Climbing Club that ventured to the cliffs annually. Nobody had ever made it to the top, and although there had been many enthusiasts over the years, there were very few members left to try.

Seeing he couldn't move in the direction he wanted to go, Aargh began again.

"Step two: Get to where I *can* go south."

Aargh knew that although they were heavily overgrown in places, the forest paths mimicked Gemini City's grid. Therefore, moving diagonally would be impossible. Even traveling in a zigzag fashion—first east, then south, then east again—would likely result in him getting stuck or turned around, so that wasn't a viable plan, either.

"I believe the best course of action," he explained to himself, "is to stick to the eastern trail until I reach the Old

Middle-Forest Road. Then, I can take it south, straight back to the Congregational House."

"That's a solid plan," Aargh replied.

"Thank you. I'm glad you think so."

"I'm wondering, though, what do you plan to do when you get there?"

"To the Congregational House?" Aargh asked.

"Yes."

"I have no idea."

"Neither do I!"

Nevertheless, Aargh felt a bit better now that he had a plan (or, at the very least, part of a plan). Instead of dwelling on what he couldn't control, he'd decided to focus on what he could manage, and his first order of business was: How can I be a better friend to Wrudge?

Wrudge would have thought this was ridiculous as Aargh was the best friend he'd ever had. From Wrudge's point of view, nothing could have made their friendship any better, but Aargh didn't know this, and he was determined to make a few changes.

"Three times a day," Aargh announced. "I'll brush Wrudge three times a day! And the very day this is all behind us, I'll make Wrudge some juicy roast lamb. I'm sure he'd love that!"

• • •

Brooding in the Marble House Nursery, the Master Prefect waited for the Wizard of the Council to return with the little girl. He was surrounded by elegant stone pillars topped with exquisite plants, making the space look more like a museum than a home. Suspended above each pillar was an oil lamp. Each lamp was encompassed by a reflector that focused a beam of light on the plant below, dramatically adding to the effect.

Sitting alone in the shadows between the pillars, the Master Prefect carefully tended his plants and pondered what TTM had told him.

Although collecting plants was a profoundly personal endeavor–considering that, for most of his life, the Master Prefect and Lord of Marble House hadn't owned much more than the shirt on his back–it also served an essential purpose. The lords and ladies, foreign dignitaries, and even members of the Council on Building Height and Adjustments who came to visit Marble House stood in awe of his collection. It was a symbol of status in the community. All of the Lords' homes had something unique. Something expensive. Something to show off at gatherings. It was less about the plants, though, as few lords knew anything at all about plants and more focused on the fact that no one could figure out how the Lord of Marble House had gotten them. It was a complete mystery, and nothing helped raise your status in society more than a good old-fashioned mystery!

The simple truth was, the Lord of Marble House was connected. Even now, he often slipped off, late at night, to visit the docks where he kept a secret office in the old Customs House. It was in a dirty, dangerous square of the district, but it was his block, and everyone left him alone.

He met with all manner of people, brokering deals and trading for his precious plants. He was good at procuring things that couldn't be sold on the open market, not even on the lowest squares of Middling Street. It was in this way that he'd learned the many secrets of Gemini City. How else could he have risen to such heights so quickly?

Usually, it took generations for homes to become available–typically, passed down from father to son. If you weren't lucky enough to have a father who owned one, it often took a lifetime for a lord to work his way up Middling Street, but he'd done it. In a few short years, he'd achieved Upper Lordship, purchased one of the high houses, and had been elected Master Prefect. Not bad for a lowly deckhand from the southern blocks. Not bad at all.

Of course, the fact that the previous lord had owed him a tidy sum of money (for something he desperately wanted to keep from the Lady of the Hall) might have greased the wheels a little. No hard feelings. It was the game of business, and the Lord of Marble House held all of the cards.

The day they'd moved in had been incredibly satisfying. He'd watched as the lords who lived south of Marble House attempted to keep up appearances, all the while secretly seething at his jumping the line, as it were. He'd survived beatings from captains and endured being talked down to by the lofty Upper Middling Street lords doing their dirty business in his office on the docks. But now, he was above them all, looking down, and it felt good.

And if someone needed a little persuading? All he had to do was pat the book he kept in his inside pocket, and they would smile, tip their hat, and wish him a good day. Knowledge was power, and the Lord of Marble House was very powerful, indeed.

He enjoyed thinking about these things on most days, but today it made him angry. One pedestal in the Nursery sat empty and not just any pedestal, either. His prized Golden

Orchid–the jewel of his collection–had been presented there. It had held pride of place before the little wizard with the absurd hat had darkened his door.

That morning had begun well enough. The Lord of Marble House had eaten a healthy breakfast, meaning large, which was his favorite kind–no more surviving on hardtack and coffee as thick as sludge for him!

He reveled in being able to eat whatever he liked. Pork sausages, guinea fowl eggs, and his favorite fish, called shinies, had been piled in front of him. He loved those crispy scales! He would pick them off one by one, watching how they shimmered in the light, and then listen as they crickle-crackled when he nibbled them like chips (but, in his estimation, infinitely better). They reminded him of where he'd come from, having hauled countless nets full of the fish in his *Before Life*, as he called it.

Marble House was much nicer than their last home–which translated to much larger–and they were still getting the lay of the land, so to speak. As he leaned back in his chair, he could hear the Lady of the House scolding a servant, "Why is this door here? It's supposed to lead to the dining room, and it's only a closet."

"Right this way, ma'am, if you please."

After several more wrong turns, the Lady of the House appeared. She wanted to discuss dismissing one of the handmaids for bringing tepid water to her bath the previous evening. She was quite perturbed, and he was eager to hear what had happened. The Lord of Marble House was always interested in hearing about people's missteps and mistakes.

"A dreadful experience," she complained. "I don't think I'll ever be able to shake off the chill. Simply dreadful! I won't have such incompetence in *my* house. I won't have it!"

The Lord of Marble House had called for the girl at once, and the lady watched with an evil grin as he sent the girl away without papers–the grubby little upstart. The pair had laughed and laughed. Then, being the refined people they were now, the lord and lady had some tea and biscuits (the tangy ones with a dollop of jam on top) to celebrate. It was always good to show everyone who was in charge.

However, the day had taken a sour turn when TTM had called them to meet with the wizard. The lord and lady left their warm tea to go to the Nursery, but the wizard wasn't there! Such audacity, making them wait. When he did arrive, he was such a disappointment!

"Couldn't he have at least tried to look the part?" they'd both asked themselves, looking at the little man with saggy robes and a ridiculously poofy hat with a giant feather on top.

"What will the neighbors think?" the Lord of Marble House had said through gritted teeth. "That's the last time I'll ever ask Pinky for wizarding advice!"

Right then and there, he'd resolved to move his cousin to a table near the kitchen. Pinky could enjoy the Marble House Ball sitting next to his in-laws while the rest of the family hobnobbed with society's elite.

What the Lord of Marble House didn't know was that Pinky (as he was known to friends after his foot had an un-fortunate run-in with a fishing net) had met with a shadowy, hooded figure the night before and was no longer attending balls or giving wizarding advice to anyone anymore.

Making the day even worse, a filthy rat had knocked over his orchid. He'd watched as his prized flower toppled off its pedestal and onto the floor with a crash. No matter what he'd tried, he couldn't save the plant. He'd even made a special ice cube and placed it gingerly on the soil, but it was no use. Each day, the plant's leaves had drooped further and further until it died.

Now, he would exact his revenge.

• • •

Stamping up the stairs, TTM called to the small room beyond the attik, "Where is my book?"

"Right where you're supposed to be, I see," he responded to himself.

Opening to a blank page, TTM began writing about the events of the day. He was going to get the last laugh where that little wizard was concerned. Of that, he was sure.

Behind a devilish grin, he thought to himself, "I wish I could be there to see the look on his face when the Wizard of the Council takes the little girl from him!"

To his surprise, this thought didn't bring him any pleasure because although he enjoyed manipulating people, he liked being there when the results of his plans came to fruition. Instead, he was sitting in his room writing about what someone else was going to do.

TTM's frustration boiled over, and, with a sharp crack, he slammed the book down, only to pull his hand back quickly, as if his fingers had been slapped with a ruler. Even though it had happened a long time ago, he vividly remembered the day he'd found Marble House's attik.

"Ow!" young TTM exclaimed.

"Serves you right!" scolded the kitchen maid. "And don't you ever think of coming in here again, or it won't be your knuckles next time. Now git!"

He was only four at the time. Hungry after a night in the stalls (having not finished his chores the previous day), he'd crept into the kitchen to search for something to eat. The moment he'd reached for one of the mouthwateringly warm, buttery biscuits...smack! The stick had come down so hard on his hand that it had been days before he could comfortably hold anything again.

As fast as he could, he'd run from the kitchen, trying to find a place to hide from his pain and humiliation. It was in that moment that he'd resolved to never finish another day without completing every last chore and to never, ever be scolded again (and he hadn't–not a single time).

During his escape, and in the farthest corner of the house, he'd found a tapestry covering the cold, stone wall. Glancing over his shoulder to see if anyone had followed him, he'd slipped behind it to hide. Much to his surprise, he found a door. It was the long-forgotten entrance to the Marble House attik.

Gemini City's building code prevented any building from being taller than two stories high, so builders often included attiks at the rear of homes for people to store all of the things they collected over the years. More often than not, owners concealed their doors behind bookcases, tapestries, or mirrors, which made them the things of legends to the people living in the poorer squares. To the affluent owners of Upper Middling Street, they were usually rooms containing old things that didn't interest them. Instead, the modern sensibility focused on what the lords referred to as *Contemporary Currency*, which was a fancy term for, "I spent too much money on this, and you should be suitably impressed."

It wasn't unusual for a family to forget they had an attik, as most people these days preferred to show off their possessions rather than hide them away. Also, the Marauders and Norters were both gone, so people didn't worry about midnight raids the way they used to. The result? Many of the highest homes had stores of precious gems or other finery hidden away for generations, forgotten with the passage of time. This was the case for Marble House, too, until TTM had found it. But now, everyone knew exactly where the attik was. However, they also knew it was where TTM lived, so people gave it a wide berth.

As with all things in Marble House, the attik was neatly cared for and filled with many wondrous things. Among TTM's favorites were the suits of armor. He kept them so carefully polished that they shined even in the dark, but that wasn't all. There were exemplary tapestries, silverware of all kinds, and even a chest filled with gemstones, just like in pirate stories.

Although TTM cared for the attik and its relic inhabitants, he didn't consider them his. He was a servant, and these things were above his station. That being said, they were in his house and, consequently, his responsibility. So, he took as much care with them as anything else in Marble House whether or not anyone saw them.

"What good are standards if you don't keep them?" TTM often told himself.

Near the back of the attik, there was a stairway that led to the roof. This intrigued the young boy because he knew that no building was allowed to be built taller than two stories high, except for the Congregational House and the Spire. To his delight, it hadn't led to the roof at all but to a small room.

The roof itself, where the gardens were kept, was raised to help with water runoff and irrigation. This meant nobody could see the little room from the roof or the street since it was neatly tucked behind the facade. It was a perfect hiding place, and it was his. It wasn't until many years later that TTM learned why the room had been built, but that was his secret, and he wasn't telling.

• • •

"That was rather fun," the Wizard of the Council cooed to himself. "Let me look at you, young Aargh...

"How delightful. And to think, I thought I would have to be clever to outwit that fool of a wizard. He wouldn't know magic if it walked up to him and introduced itself. What do you think of that, little girl?" he asked the bundle of robes, but there was no answer.

She didn't trust this man because he didn't feel like her wizard. This man was shallow, like a mirror. It was similar to seeing the reflection of a room you were standing in but knowing you couldn't reach in because it was only a thin piece of glass. She felt that if someone knew how, they could shatter that glass and reveal the real person behind the disguise. The problem was, she couldn't figure out what was hidden behind the reflection, and she didn't want to find out either. So, she stayed quiet.

"No matter," the wizard was saying. "I don't need you to speak. I only need your magic."

The wizard moved easily through the forest, making a bee-line straight for the Congregational House. His triumphant return would begin with a grand entrance. The Wizard of the Council was exceptionally good at grand entrances, and he enjoyed them immensely. He would throw open the Grand Rotunda doors and stride in with the little girl to the Master Prefect's astonishment.

It wouldn't be as grand as the day he'd arrived in Gemini City, though. What an excellent idea it had been to borrow that theatrical carriage! Cutting edge stuff and, with some magic of his own, it had made quite the impression. However, since it wasn't proper to wear the same gown to more than one ball, he was always on the lookout for new ways to make an entrance. But, then again, few things in life work out as we hope or plan.

To the Wizard of the Council's supreme disappointment, they entered the Grand Rotunda to nothing more than complete silence.

"He's probably home brooding over his ridiculous flowers," the wizard said to the vacant room as he put down the child. Of course, this was precisely what the Master Prefect was doing.

Composing himself, the wizard surveyed the venerated space. Slowly, he began skirting the outer wall, passing the polished black marble pillars that encircled the room. They jutted out of the floor like barren tree trunks, stripped of their branches and foliage. He touched their cold surfaces with the tips of his fingers as he passed. In between the bare trunks were smug-looking busts of past Master Prefects.

"How arrogant they all look," he mused. "They knew nothing of real power."

The wizard turned and started walking back toward the center of the room. Long rows of arced stone desks followed the contour of the curved walls. This was where the Upper and Lower Lords used to address the Master Prefect. Now they sat unused and gathering dust. Cold. Lifeless.

In the center of the room was the Master Prefect's chair. It was a powerful-looking stone chair with gold and silver inlay. As he sat down on the cushioned seat, the wizard ran his fingers along the armrests, tracing the intricate inlaid filigree.

"Now, little girl, it's time for a test. Let's see if we make a good team," he said menacingly.

She shrank back from him, recoiling from his outstretched hand.

"I'm looking forward to giving the Master Prefect his little demonstration and then showing him who actually holds the power in this city."

People stopped what they were doing and looked up as an ominous boom rumbled across Ardilakk valley.

"That's strange," they thought. "Not a single cloud in the sky. Better bring in the chickens."

Aargh had just reached the old road when he heard the thunder echo across the valley. He recognized the sensation from his experience at Aldenthwaine's hut. There was magic in the air. Aargh could feel it.

"The wizard is practicing," Aargh said to himself, "and if this is practice, what will come next?"

That thought made him shudder, and Aargh wished Wrudge was there with him just as he'd always been since their days at wizarding school.

"No, no, of course not young Aargh," answered Professor Aldenthwaine. "You aren't harming your familiar by using its magic. Think of it more as sharing. Class, do you hear the concern in Aargh's voice? You should all love your familiar as he does. They aren't tools to be used. No, no. They are your companions. You're a team, and together, you'll do more extraordinary things than you could possibly do alone.

"Whether they be the crayfish in the stream or birds in the sky, whether it helps pollinate plants or honors us by serving as sustenance for our bodies, even if it is merely pretty to look at, all living things are special and must be respected. Just because something can't build buildings or communicate the way we can, that doesn't mean they are any less valuable to the world.

"In the end, we're no stronger or wiser than any other living thing as we too will return to the earth to continue the never-ending Great Cycle."

Usually, Aargh relaxed when he thought about his beloved mentor's wise lessons but not today. Instead, it only made him miss Wrudge more.

"Where could he be?" he wondered, trying not to think the worst, but no, Aargh was sure he still felt a connection to his familiar. It just felt far away. Muted. Distant.

For a brief moment, that thought gave Aargh hope, but then, he realized with a jolt, he *had* seen magic! His connection to Wrudge was obviously magical. Why hadn't he ever thought about it that way before? Aargh began questioning everything he could remember. Finally, he focused on one memory: the giant balls in front of Marble House. Yes! He'd seen magic there, too.

Aargh remembered studying the sky, reflected as clear as day, on one of the balls. He'd marveled at the clouds moving across its surface, converging with the buildings as they rounded the curved horizon. Then he'd looked far down Middling Street, stretching out to his left and right. He could see people and carriages on the street, distorted by the sphere, and…and…he saw his beloved mentor. Aldenthwaine was standing right behind him! At the time, Aargh had shaken it off as nothing more than a mirage created by the sun, but it had been him. He was sure of it. And Aldenthwaine was beckoning to him!

"Oh," Aargh moaned. Not only had he seen Aldenthwaine, but his mentor had been calling out to him. The more Aargh thought about it, the more he realized Aldenthwaine had been trying to reach him for years. So many times, Aargh had brushed off the things he'd seen as a mere trick of the light. Magic had always surrounded him, but he'd been so convinced it didn't exist that he couldn't see it. Now it was too late.

Slowly, Aargh became aware that magic wasn't the only thing that had evaded his notice. It was as if he'd only been able to see what he'd expected to see. Without realizing it, he'd become like his professors, unable to see past what they already knew and entirely blind to the realities of the world around them.

Aargh felt very small, drowning in an ocean of his own ignorance. He was a student again, and this time, he wouldn't close his mind to the unexplained. From now on, he would immerse himself in anything he didn't immediately understand because that was obviously where magic had hidden from him. Unfortunately, that couldn't undo the past. The Wizard of the Council had easily used Aargh's love for his mentor to deceive him.

"What a fool I am," Aargh scolded himself. "How could I not see through his disguise?"

Aargh, the novice, was only beginning to learn about such things. He didn't know that love is always blind, shrouded by a veil of acceptance and forgiveness. However, if that veil is brushed aside, love can turn to fury in an instant. Aargh could feel the anger of betrayal building, pushing him to do something rash. He'd better be careful, or he might make a critical mistake.

"Calm down," he told himself. "Remember your *C's*. Remember your *C's*. Deep, cleansing breaths…*Calm Your Heart*…relax and think of a safe place…*Clear Your Mind*… and above all else, *Concentration is Key*."

But it was no use. All Aargh could concentrate on was, "Is she okay?"

Aargh began to walk.

"Why did the Wizard of the Council take her?"

He began to jog.

"She's my responsibility. She needs me."

The trees began to speed by.

"Wrudge, Wrudge! Where are you? I need you!"

Chapter 8

I KNOW YOUR SECRET

Rage coursed through his veins as TTM paced back and forth like a caged animal.

"Who does that wizard think he is? This is *my* house, with *my* rules, and no one sends me to the basement to watch over a little girl. No one!"

"I know your secret," a voice, gentle as a warm summer breeze rustling the leaves of the ancient oaks in the forest, whispered in his ear.

TTM stumbled ever so slightly but continued to pace back and forth, still fuming. If it wasn't for his overwhelming sense of responsibility, TTM would have refused, but instead, he did as he was instructed. This was one time he wished he didn't have such high standards.

"This is entirely outrageous! Little girls are the handmaid's responsibility, *not*–I repeat–*not* the responsibility of the Head Butler!"

Moments earlier, the Wizard of the Council had marched them both down to the basement and seated the little girl right on top of a case of the finest vintage.

The finest vintage!

Wasn't a case of the watered-down house wine good enough for sitting?…the junk he served the *connoisseurs* upstairs who went on and on saying things like, "Oh, yes. Mmm. I remember being introduced to this fine wine at the Ruby Mark Gala last year. The Upper Lords only serve the finest wines. It has such a fragrant bouquet, like flowers in springtime, ha, ha, ha."

"Imbeciles!" TTM grumbled to himself.

TTM knew what a fine wine was. He'd spent many quiet hours in the wine cellar sampling the wines he'd purchased for the house. That was where he practiced the Fivers, as he called them: see, swirl, sniff, sip, and savor. The last was his personal favorite, and he couldn't wait to try it out on this new case, but a little girl was sitting on it!

The voice came again, "I know your secret," and a shiver ran down TTM's spine.

What an indignity! He couldn't take it anymore. Strung up as tight as a piano wire, TTM snapped.

"Enough of this!" he barked, whirling on the stone door and glaring into the wine cellar.

He fully intended to scold the little girl, but when their eyes met, she didn't look away. TTM's breath caught in his throat as he looked through the door's small window. She wasn't looking away. In fact, she was staring right at him!

"Look away," TTM commanded himself. "Look away, right now!" but he couldn't.

Only one other person had ever looked into his eyes that way before. Most people did everything in their power *not* to look into TTM's steely gray eyes. His parents used to study the floor or look out a window when they spoke to him. The callers to Marble House often looked up and down Middling Street. The Lord of the House didn't even look him directly in the eyes, but the little girl did. It felt as if she was burrowing right down into his soul. Even so, he couldn't look away.

Then, TTM felt something strange in his stomach. It felt like butterflies fluttering around.

"How did they get in there?" he wondered absently, and his feet began to sweat.

TTM looked through the strong stone door at the little girl, and his shoulders began to sag. It was as if he'd been carrying a heavy weight over a long distance–which of course, he had.

"You're a wizard," she said quietly.

Her words landed on TTM with the force of a falling boulder. He fell forward, placing both hands on the door to steady himself. It wasn't that she knew his secret. It was that no one had ever seen him as anything other than a servant before. All his life, he'd dreamed about teaching history at the Gemini City School of Wizarding. However, he'd been born into the world of service, and that, as they say, was that. Like his father (and his father's father before him), TTM was part of Marble House's workings, and that was where he would stay whether he liked it or not.

Everyone who came to the house marveled at its beauty, with its polished marble hallways, finely decorated sitting rooms, and grand courtyard. The exquisite horticultural displays, carefully tended by the Lord of the House, always produced the desired effect.

Yet, to TTM, Marble House felt more like a prison than a palace, and it made him bitter. Day in and day out, he greeted people as they came and went but not TTM. There he stayed, confined by the smooth, cold stone that surrounded him. Instead of looking out and seeing the wonders of the world, all he saw was himself trapped in the infinite reflections of the tall mirrors that lined the hallways. Every time he passed one, it reminded him that no matter what door he passed through or what window he looked out of, he was stuck forever between the stoic stone walls of Marble House. Interestingly, it was something his father used to say that had unwittingly given him the idea to expand his knowledge, even if he couldn't expand his world.

"If you learn nothing else from me, learn this," his father would say. "To be the best you can be, you must pay attention to every detail. Know what your lord wants before he asks for it. Know what his guests need before they arrive, and most importantly, never put your needs before your betters."

TTM took this advice to heart in more ways than his father had ever known. Not only had he paid attention to his father and the lords, but he'd also paid attention to everything around him. No detail ever went unnoticed, and that was how he'd learned to talk to the old oak tree of Marble House.

She was an elegant tree, and she loved to talk. TTM would never forget the first time she answered him. She poured out her stories to him so quickly that TTM thought he might drown. But with practice, he soon learned to follow her roots, focusing on what he wanted to know. Whereas the wizards who visited the house were always looking to the future, TTM was fascinated by the past. He wanted to know everything he could about the history of Gemini City.

Beginning when he was a child, he would slip away and talk to the tree. Over time, they developed quite a rapport. He would listen as she told him about the workings of the world, and in return, she'd listen to him relate all that happened in the house and on Middling Street. She'd lived so long in the courtyard, with no other trees around, that she was beginning to feel out of touch.

The old tree of Marble House longed to be surrounded by the silly musings of saplings swaying in the wind or to hear the ancient voices of the elder trees. She pined for the open sky above her and the flowing green forest that filled Ardilakk Valley.

Also trapped by the house's walls, one might say, TTM understood how she felt. They'd spent many wonderful hours together, and over time, TTM became the most knowledgeable person in all of Gemini City, but he'd never dared to say his secret out loud—not a single time in his entire life.

"How does she know?" TTM asked himself, but before he could answer, a sharp voice interrupted his thoughts.

"What is going on here?" the Wizard of the Council demanded, pushing TTM aside.

TTM was so startled that he didn't even remember to tell *BoB* about the incident. In fact, TTM never wrote another entry into either of his little black books ever again. He simply backed away, still reeling from her words echoing in his ears.

"There you are," the Wizard of the Council said in a menacing tone. "Time to go upstairs for our *demonstration*."

Something about the way the wizard had said *demonstration* shook TTM, and he started to feel something he hadn't felt in a very long time: worry.

The Wizard pointed at the door, and TTM unlocked it. The heavy marble door swung open, balanced perfectly on its well-oiled hinges. TTM would never have a squeaky hinge in *his* house, especially the wine cellar door.

"Come with me!" the wizard demanded, and the little girl climbed down off of the best vintage.

As they left the room, she slipped her hand into TTM's hand. He looked down into her sad chocolatey brown eyes and gave her hand a little squeeze. Then, they walked to the courtyard together.

• • •

"Wrudge! It's time! Hurry!" Aargh called out frantically as he raced down Middling Street.

Silent as the grave, the Congregational House loomed ominously in the gloom–its doors left open by the crazed wizard who was now rushing down the street screaming for his rat as dark clouds began gathering above Marble House.

People slammed their doors and shuttered their windows. No one wanted to get in the way of a wizard who had gone off the deep end. It didn't matter if there was one spell in the world or a hundred; either way, the Footman would be coming, and that meant it was time to head indoors. How were they to know the Footman was permanently off-duty after being carried to the sheriff's office, where he was sleeping off the mother of all hangovers in City Cell #1?

"Another one's lost it," Aargh heard an old tinker say as he covered his tinkling cart.

"Maybe I *have* lost it. I've lost everything else, after all. I couldn't see magic, even when it was staring me in the face. My career is in ruins. I have no idea how I could possibly return to the Spire now. I've lost Wrudge, and worst of all, I couldn't stop the Wizard of the Council from taking our precious little girl. One time, just one time, I would like to get something right."

Unfortunately, Aargh realized that was unlikely, considering he had no idea what to do when he got to Marble House (let alone how to deal with the wizard).

A brilliant flash of lightning lit up the street, and Aargh looked up. He watched as clouds began spreading across the sky toward the horizon. Time was quickly running out.

"Wrudge!"

• • •

By law, all legislative decisions had to be voted on in the Congregational House chambers. Therefore, to say a request to attend a legislative ceremony at Marble House was out of the ordinary would have been a gross understatement. However, since no member of the legislature had met with the Master Prefect since being barred from the Grand Rotunda, they came anyway.

There they stood, the twelve Upper Lords of Gemini City, uncomfortably milling around the Marble House courtyard. The invitation had instructed them to wear the robes of their station and not to be late. None of them had any idea why they were there. Some imagined they were getting an award, and one or two hoped there might be cake after the ceremony. When it started to get darker, a few began to murmur about the threatening clouds forming overhead. There was, however, one thing they agreed upon: they were all glad it wasn't raining, at least, not yet. This, in and of itself, was notable, as they had never come to a consensus about anything before.

On the Wizard of the Council's recommendation, the Master Prefect had already disbanded the Lower House of Lords, but these men weren't too worried. They represented Gemini City's wealthiest, most influential families and were reasonably confident their positions were secure. This was true, of course, but not in the way they were thinking.

The gathered lords could hear deep rumblings high in the sky above, and it unsettled them. The tree in the courtyard cast a dark, bluish shadow on the ground, and the pillars that held up the archways surrounding the space looked more like prison bars than polished marble in the shadowy gloaming. The air felt thick and heavy around them.

With his characteristic flourish, the wizard entered the courtyard, followed by a pale little girl. The lords exchanged questioning looks as this was highly irregular! Why was there a little girl at their meeting?

TTM–having been instructed to stay out of the way– watched uneasily from the shadows.

"Through the unassailable wisdom of our leader and following my sage counsel, today will be the dawn of a new era for Gemini City!" the wizard boomed, his voice echoing down the long halls of Marble House.

The wizard then raised his hand over his head and bowed low as the Master Prefect entered the courtyard. The Upper Lords clapped politely.

The Master Prefect nodded to the wizard, and a flash of lightning shattered the night sky, reflected all around them by the mirrors that lined the walls. The shock of the moment rattled the once-proud Upper Lords, and the color drained from their faces. They began shuffling closer to each other, never taking their eyes off of the wizard.

The Master Prefect was pleased. He enjoyed exerting power over the people around him, and this was going far better than even he had hoped it would. As the light flickered off his gilded robes, the Master Prefect stood there, confident his plans were coming to fruition and having no idea whatsoever that nothing could have been farther from the truth. Soon, he would see the folly of his ways.

"No more will the people of Gemini City be weighed down by the faults of their forefathers," the wizard continued, his voice growing in power. "No more will history anchor everyone to the past. No more will every home contain a reminder of history's failings, preventing Gemini City from setting sail on the sea of the future. Freedom is what I am speaking about, and that freedom from the past starts today!"

With that, the Wizard of the Council lowered his wand and called out, "Inter ligna silvarum!" and the Great Tree of the Courtyard erupted in flames.

A sharp pang of realization shot through the Master Prefect as he watched the old oak burn—the flickering light illuminating the contorted face of the Wizard of the Council. He'd always prided himself on being able to read every situation and every person. Not once had he ever been bested in a deal or been caught off guard before, until now.

With the same sensation as if he was lifting his head out of the water, the Master Prefect's mind began to clear. He could hear the screams of terror coming from the twelve Lords of the Upper House as they tried to escape the courtyard. He, too, felt the urge to flee, but there was no place to go. A hundred Palace Guardesmen had appeared, stepping into every archway that surrounded the courtyard, trapping them like rats on a sinking ship. The venerable Lords of Gemini City piled together in a corner of the courtyard clamoring for a safety they would never achieve.

"Bow down to your new Master," the wizard bellowed. "Bow down and ask for my mercy!"

TTM watched as his dearest friend in all of the world burned with the wizard's fire. He could feel her pain, and it pierced his heart like a knife. Then, as silent as a shadow passing in the night and as invisible as a summer breeze, TTM whisked the child out of the courtyard. No one noticed, for no one ever noticed TTM when he didn't want to be noticed, not even the Palace Guarde. They were all too busy bowing to the false king.

Chapter 9

THE DEATH OF THE WAND

Embers slowly danced in the air like fireflies on a calm summer's eve, belying the terror unfolding in the courtyard of Marble House. Smoke billowed from the center of the building, towering high in the air as black clouds spread across the sky toward the horizon. All of the houses on Upper Middling Street were dark. Their inhabitants were too terrified to do anything other than cower in stairwells, basements, and wine cellars. No one even called the Dousemen, not that they would have come, as word of something terrible happening at the high houses had traveled rapidly through the city–something involving wizards that shouldn't be meddled with until it passed.

With phantom-like stealth, TTM appeared out of the shadows, stepping directly into Aargh's way. Shocked by TTM's sudden appearance, Aargh stumbled to a stop.

"Get out of my way!" Aargh howled with a mixture of suffering and conviction. "You can't stop me! I'm here for the child. Where is she?"

Towering above the ex-wizard, TTM looked quizzically at Aargh. He admired Aargh's loyalty to the little girl and his determination to help her no matter what the consequences. It was a little like the pride TTM took in running Marble House, and, in his own way, he could relate to what Aargh felt. TTM realized that he might have misjudged the disheveled wizard, and then, for only the second time in his entire life, TTM found himself looking up to someone.

It was a bright, cold Midswinter day when an awkward-looking man in a tweed jacket had come to call on the 13th Lord of Marble House. TTM's father had answered the door and shown the man into the study. There, he'd carefully laid out many maps and diagrams all over the lord's private desk.

Throughout the afternoon and well into the night, the two men had pored over the documents. Hidden in a dark corner of the room, TTM had watched and listened, but he couldn't make out what they were saying. The man in the tweed coat appeared to be showing the 13th Lord of Marble House the location of something north of the Once-Great Wall, but that was all he'd been able to glean from their conversation. TTM's attention had been entirely focused on the papers.

Just as TTM started to think he'd better get to bed, an opportunity presented itself. The two men left the room, and he slipped out of the shadows to take a closer look at the papers. They were so detailed! Expertly crafted blueprints, masterfully drawn renderings, and his favorite, detailed maps of the city were all spread across the stone-topped desk. The documents filled his eyes and mind with wonder. One by one, TTM had moved the oversized sheets of paper around the desk to get a better look.

Lost in his thoughts, TTM was startled when a voice came from behind him, "I-I thought you might want to take a-a look," the awkward-looking man stammered. "I-I saw you watching from o-over there. Impressive, a-aren't they?"

TTM had slowly and carefully tried to recede into the shadows, hoping to slip away before the Lord returned. He wasn't used to callers on the house noticing him, let alone looking at him. Truthfully, TTM couldn't remember anyone ever looking directly into his eyes that way before.

The man seemed to read his mind and said, "Don't worry. I-It's just u-us. The lord has gone o-out. I-I was going to put these a-away, but I-I would be happy to show them to you. Would you like to see?"

TTM nodded and took a step closer to the desk—his fingers lightly touching the cold, smooth surface. He listened with all of his heart as the man spoke. Every word was a revelation; each thought a door opening to a new world waiting to be discovered. TTM had never met a teacher before. He'd never gone to school or even sat in a classroom. His lessons usually consisted of things like "Stay out of the way!" or "Bring this to your father now, boy!" and TTM wanted more, so much more!

TTM wanted to be like this man. He longed to learn everything there was to know about their city. He wanted to see the buildings expertly designed by ancient craftsmen without the need for mortar or modern technologies. He wanted to learn Gemini City's history, how the River Wide fueled their economy, what secrets were hidden in the

Northern Forest, and why the Great Mount Ardilakk had never been scaled.

But most importantly, TTM wanted to share the knowledge he'd learned with others the way the teacher had so willingly done for him. Maybe someday he would, but today, he had other responsibilities that required his attention.

Thinking about the man who'd shown kindness to him so many years ago, TTM silently moved to the side, revealing the little girl concealed behind him. She ran to Aargh, throwing herself into his arms.

"I knew you'd come," she whispered.

Aargh breathed out a sigh of relief so long it was as if he'd been holding his breath ever since the clearing. However, Aargh was also deeply confused by what was happening. Why was she with the butler from Marble House? And why were they on the street? Aargh was feeling even smaller than he usually did, standing there with a menacing storm gathering overhead and TTM looking down at him. So, he did the only thing he could think of doing. Aargh gently put the girl down, took a step forward, and reached out his arm to thank TTM.

As thunder rumbled through the stone city, rain began to fall, sizzling as it struck the embers drifting in the air around them. The two men stood, arms locked and eyes fixed. Both were feeling a sense of relief more profound than either had ever known.

With a terrible crash, a bolt of lightning struck the center of Marble House. All of the doors and windows exploded outward, covering the street with dust and rubble. They shielded their heads and ducked behind a stone parceldrop box for cover.

From out of the devastation stepped the Wizard of the Council. His spectacular white robes stood out against the shattered walls of the once noble house. In his hand was the wand and around his neck was the golden seal of the Master Prefect.

Aargh didn't hesitate.

"She's your responsibility, now. No matter what happens, you must protect her."

TTM nodded and offered his hand to the little girl.

Aargh gave her a squeeze and whispered in her ear, "You're mine, and I will never let anything bad happen to you. Do you understand? I promise."

Her eyes grew wide as saucers, and she hugged him back with all of her might. Then, in an instant, TTM whisked her away to safety, and they were gone.

Standing alone before the Wizard of the Council, there would be no safety for Aarghathlain the Novice, Student of the World, and Keeper of the Precious Child.

"Give her to me, little boy!" the Wizard of the Council commanded, the air electric with magic. "She's no longer your concern."

It's amazing how many thoughts can pass through your mind in a brief moment, and suddenly, Aargh was back in school, standing next to Groundsman Grimms' desk.

"Give it to me, little boy. Give it to me right now," Grimms was demanding. "Nobody snoops around the Private Spire Garden without my permission. Do you hear me? Nobody. Especially not students!"

Aargh looked away. He could see the other boys having fun playing games and fooling around outside. The office felt dark and oppressive. It wasn't the first time he'd been held back, and it wouldn't be the last.

"Well, what are you waiting for? Didn't you hear me? Give it to me!" the man demanded again in a harsh tone.

Hesitantly, Aargh reached out his boyish hand and slowly opened his fingers. On his palm was a rather impressive beetle. Its shiny, iridescent carapace reflected a myriad of colors in the boy's eyes as he looked down at it.

"No one goes where they aren't supposed to in *my* school," he said, and with one swift stroke, the Head Groundsman slapped Aargh's hand.

"Let that be a lesson to you. Stay out of the Private Spire garden!" Grimms snapped.

The young boy gingerly closed his hand as a single tear slid silently down his cheek.

"No! You can't have her!" he screamed, but the wizard was no longer paying attention to Aargh.

The Wizard of the Council had a strange look on his face. Following his gaze, Aargh became aware that they weren't alone. He felt a tiny hand slip into his, and he lovingly looked down at the child, understanding there was nothing he *wouldn't*…no, nothing he *couldn't* do for her.

"We won't let anything happen to you either," she said, giving his hand a little squeeze.

In her other hand was TTM, standing defiantly and staring at the Wizard of the Council. At Aargh's feet was his trusty familiar, and Wrudge had brought reinforcements.

Filling the street, covering the rooftops, pouring out of every alleyway, and on every sill and stoop were thousands—no, tens of thousands—of rats. Their hair was standing on end, pulsing with a glow as golden as an autumn sunrise, and their eyes were burning as red as hot coals. Slowly, their pulsating became synchronized, and as it did, Aargh's eyes began to glow, too. Rats are communal creatures; therefore, if you're connected to one, you're connected to the entire colony.

There Aargh stood, one with every rat in Gemini City. They were the most powerful familiar ever to be commanded by a wizard, but Aargh didn't yet comprehend the magical door that had been opened for him. The Wizard of the Council, being more versed in the ways of magic, understood what was happening and began to retreat as quickly as possible. He cast spell after spell after spell, shattering the facades of the once-great halls of Upper Middling Street.

"I don't know what to do!" Aargh yelled as he took off after the wizard.

Followed by a wave of rats pouring out onto the street, Aargh called out, "Little One, I need your help. I need you to stop time. You know, the way you did when the Footman came. Will you do that for me?"

"I didn't stop time," she replied as they ran ahead of the river of rats flooding the street behind them.

"Slow it down then. Make us move faster. Do something...anything...please! I need to catch up to the Wizard of the Council."

"I can't do those things. I'm not a wizard."

Without warning, Aargh abruptly stopped running, skidding to a halt right in the middle of the street.

"Not a wizard?"

That didn't make sense. She definitely was a wizard. There was no doubt about it. He'd seen it with his own eyes. Then Aargh realized something. She must be terrified. All he had to do was help her calm down. Then, he was confident she would be able to help.

Taking a deep breath, Aargh knelt down before the child, and as he did, TTM and the rats gathered around them.

"I know this is very scary, but this is not the time for games. I need your help. Whatever you did that day, do it again for me, please?"

"I only asked for help," she said innocently. "And you helped me."

Aargh felt dizzy as realization began to dawn on his awakening mind. He didn't know how but it had been *him* on the steps of Marble House, making time slow down. It had been *him* whisking his friends to safety from the Footman. It had been *him*.

"I am the wizard," he said, almost laughing at the thought. "…a wizard."

Aargh wheeled around and locked his eyes on the Wizard of the Council. He was destroying their world. He was destroying *her* world, and Aargh *couldn't* let that happen. No, he *would not* let that happen. It was time to put an end to all of this.

Countless fiery red eyes blazed all around Aargh, fixed intently on the newly reinstated wizard. There was a palpable sense of anticipation in the air. What was he going to do?

Aargh slowly raised his fists above his head, and a silence fell over Middling Street. All of the rats stood perfectly still, their hair standing on end, crackling with magic. Aargh became aware of the energy surging around them. He reached out to it with his mind–tentatively at first but with growing confidence–and called it to him. With the force of a mighty river descending from the mountains, Aargh began to feel the energy flow through him.

There, in the middle of the street, Aargh stood motionless as the cool rain fell on his outstretched arms and upturned face. Illuminated by flashes of lightning in the sky, Aargh remained still and calm.

Slowly, he lowered his head and opened his eyes. Then, Aarghathlain *the Wizard* opened his hands, and the street erupted with light! It was as if a million stars had dropped from the heavens at his command, and Aargh ran.

The world melted into a blur as he hurtled toward the Wizard of the Council. Nothing could stop him, and nothing could get in his way. Raindrops slowed to a stop, lightning froze in long crooked streaks in the sky, and like an avalanche crashing down from the high mountain peaks, Aargh collided with the wizard. They crashed to the ground, and the wand skidded away across the stony street.

Aargh looked directly into the wizard's eyes and saw behind the reflection. The Wizard of the Council was no wizard! He was something older, more dangerous. Aargh didn't comprehend who or what the man was, but he knew one thing with absolute certainty: the Wizard of the Council's magic didn't belong to him, and Aargh wasn't going to let him keep it.

The two powerful men scuffled and shoved, trying to reach the fallen wand. Each fist landed with the force of rolling boulders, and each bolt of lightning scarred the once-smooth Middling Street homes.

Aargh knew that retrieving the wand was his only hope of stopping the crazed maniac from leveling their city, but he didn't get there first. Both men grabbed it at the same time. Thunder boomed, and sparks rained down as the wizard and the imposter struggled for control of the wand. There was so much energy in the air that a magical haze made the street look otherworldly, the light bending and refracting the way a mirage floats above the horizon on a hot summer day.

As his connection with the rats grew stronger, Aargh could feel primal emotions awakening in him. Aargh let out a howl, and, in response, the street filled with a thunderous chorus of rats screeching, hissing, and chattering. The imposter realized this was a battle he couldn't win, at least not this time. He'd risen from the earth before, and he would rise again. But for now, it was time to go.

"You think you're so powerful, little wizard? You know nothing of power! And, if I can't be the One True Wizard, no one will be!"

With that, the Wizard of the Council thrust his knee between their hands and bellowed, "Ardeat et mundi!"

Aargh could feel the wood fracture and split as the wand's power was released in one vast magical blast. Everyone was knocked off their feet, and the Wizard of the Council shot straight up into the air.

Weary and sore, Aargh clawed his way to TTM, Wrudge, and the collapsed bundle of robes. Soaked by the falling rain, he cradled her in his arms.

"Are you hurt, my sweet girl?"

She gave no response. Gone were the giggles of happier times, and her skin looked cold and gray against the wet, black stones of the street beneath them. Obscured by the falling rain, a single tear slid down the wizard's face.

Brushing her hair aside, he leaned down and kissed her forehead, whispering, "Have you forgotten what I told you? You're mine, Little One, and I will never let anything bad happen to you. Nothing. Not a single thing."

The bundle opened her eyes and asked, "Not ever?"

"No. Not ever. Are you okay?"

"I'm not so bad," she said, but her face told a very different story as she stared into the sky.

Following her gaze, they all looked up to see the Wizard of the Council riding the blast high into the clouds. Everyone watched in horror as he burst into flames—a ring of fire spreading across the sky.

Chapter 10

THE ONE TRUE
BOOK OF SPELLS

Ash clouds rolled like banks of fog across the city. Aargh's mouth gaped, and his lungs burned as he breathed in the toxic, smoke-filled air. No matter how hard he tried, he couldn't focus. Everything looked hazy and muted; that is, everything except for the raging inferno that engulfed the forest. Ferocious and insatiable, it was devouring all of the trees and oxygen around them. Aargh couldn't shake the feeling that this night would end in impenetrable darkness.

Moments earlier, a wave of magical fire had traveled out from the city in all directions, burning every tree in its path and driving the rats and other animals underground to safety. Powerless to stop it, the night watchmen had clung to their posts in abject terror as their eyes followed the path of the fire speeding through the forest and beyond. Soon, every tree would be ablaze–the mountains surrounding them jutting out of the earth like fiery fingers reaching into the sky.

Terrifying screams filled Aargh's thoughts, and he held onto his head as if it might explode.

"The trees! Oh, the trees!" he moaned, every other thought in his mind blotted out by the wailing of the forest. "They're being cooked alive! Splitting and cracking! Tumbling to the forest floor!"

For the first time in his wizarding life, Aargh heard all of the trees speaking with only one voice; one thought; one plea, "Help us, please!"

Their combined cries were slamming into every wizard's mind with a force that threatened to drive them all mad.

Behind them lay the city in ruin, and before them, the forest was erupting like a volcano, not of liquid stone but of living branches and bark. Had it not been so incomprehensibly terrifying, it might have been almost beautiful—yellows, oranges, and reds playing against the pitch-black sky like a serene autumn sunset, but there was no chill in the air.

The heat was so intense that it repelled the city dwellers' advances, turning their metal carriages into rolling ovens. Nothing could stem the tsunami of destruction washing across the countryside. The very earth shook beneath their feet, and the suffering was palpable.

Once-stoic wizards flailed in the scorching wind or writhed in agony on the ground. Some cried out, trying to cast spells they didn't know, while others hid from the onslaught, whimpering at their magical impotence.

Their world was burning, and so was their world's history. One tree at a time, everyone's stories were being erased along with their keepers. No more could the story of a house's lineage be told by the grand old tree in the courtyard. No more could the wizards of the day follow the One True Root to foretell the future. And most importantly, no more, on a bright summer's morn, could you sit with your back against your favorite tree's trunk and look up at the gently rustling leaves, watching the sun peek through the branches.

"Oh!" Aargh moaned again, unaware that four small hands were helping to steady him. Two hands, containing all the love in the world, gently held his side, and two little (and rather sharp) hands gripped his right calf so tightly that the tiny claws drew blood. Wrudge had crawled under Aargh's robes to get as close as possible to the wizard. This was *his* moment.

Wrudge had always known this time would come. It wasn't a secret. Everyone knew the third rule of wizarding: *Be prepared to be remarkable.* True, he hadn't known what it meant until this moment, but it was the price of being a familiar, and Wrudge didn't hesitate.

As he gripped Aargh's leg, he thought about the time they'd spent together. He remembered the day when Aargh failed his first year wizarding exam because he'd been distracted by the feathery ends of the roots. Aargh had predicted it would rain, even as they all stood under a bright blue cloudless sky. That was before Aargh had started wearing fancy oversized robes and a feather on top of his hat. He was still a young wizard studying the *Art of Rooting* by Thistlebright the Wise (a renowned wizard and founding member of the school), but even back then, Aargh was kind. Distracted? Yes. So focused on his studies that he didn't notice which shoe he was putting on which foot? Yes. But also unfailingly kind.

Young Wrudge, feeling a little peckish, had been exploring a bit of moldy cheese when a shop owner noticed him sniffing around. Aargh had seen it all. He'd rushed over to see if Wrudge, who had taken a nasty kick to his side, was okay. Aargh had gingerly picked up the injured rat and deftly hid him under his novice's cloak.

Over the next few weeks, Aargh had carefully nursed Wrudge back to health. When he'd started to feel better, and after a nice bowl of warm milk, Aargh had gotten serious one night and pulled up a chair, seating himself right in front of Wrudge. Aargh had a rather pensive look on his face, and Wrudge, being an exceptionally clever rat, knew exactly what he was going to say. It was going to be a day to remember!

Slowly, Aargh began, "Listen, Wrudge. I know you've been through a lot, so you don't have to answer right away. I've been thinking about things, and well, right now, I'm not an accomplished wizard. I know that, really, I do, but someday I will be. Accomplished, I mean, or I hope to be, and I need someone I can trust by my side. I don't know if you know this, but a wizard is only as strong as the bond with his familiar. It won't be easy. We'll have to work hard, and it will take time, but we'll get there, I know it.

"I have to warn you, though: there's a price. All wizards and familiars are required to *Be prepared to be remarkable.* I'll be honest. I don't know what that means yet, but I imagine we may be called on to do something extraordinary someday. The other boys say it's just there to scare young wizards, but I think it might mean something very important.

"So, do you think you can do that? Will you be my familiar? And, most importantly, can you be remarkable?"

Wrudge was a young rat then and somewhat perky, you might say. His fur was positively electric with excitement, and, without a second thought, he leapt right into Aargh's arms. The deal was settled. Aargh and Wrudge would travel the world of magic together.

Truth be told, it was everything Wrudge had hoped it would be and much more. Aargh did become exceptional, and through it all, trusty Wrudge was always by his side. They'd visited palatial homes and, even better, sampled the most delightful (and such decadent) food! No rat had ever had it better.

True, being the only rat familiar, sometimes people said mean things to him or made him stay outside, but Aargh always treated him with respect. They were a team, and one of the responsibilities of being on that team was that they would have to be remarkable one day.

That day was today, and Wrudge was ready.

The heat was unbearable. Even through Aargh's robes, Wrudge's whiskers began to singe, but that didn't stop him. He leaned into Aargh's leg with every ounce of his strength and began to glow, shining brighter than any rat had ever shined before.

Wrudge glowed because this was the promise he'd made. He glowed because he would fulfill that promise no matter what the cost, and he glowed because he was, without question, a trustworthy rat. But above all else, Wrudge glowed because he loved Aargh. Aargh was his best friend in all of the world, and right now, Aargh needed him to be remarkable. So, Wrudge puffed himself up, pouring everything he could into his glow, and then...

Wrudge gave his glow to Aargh.

As it passed into the wizard, the world began to fade to black. Wrudge heard Aargh cry out, and he knew it had worked. He'd given Aargh enough magic to overcome the earsplitting cries of the trees.

Wrudge felt a kind hand reach down and gently lift him up. The last thing he ever heard was his best friend's voice saying, "You did it, old friend. You were truly remarkable," and Wrudge was happy.

• • •

"Little girl! Please, come back!"

TTM watched Aargh and the little girl disappear into the crowd as he was washed away by the people flowing through the streets like the Fortnight Flood that had wiped out the lowest blocks of Old Westie Sowt generations before.

"To this day, some buildings still have high water marks etched into their corners," TTM thought.

Catching himself, TTM scolded, "What a stupid thing to think about at a time like this!"

"But is it?" he wondered. "With all of the trees burning, someone is going to have to remember the past, or it will be lost forever. Why not me?"

However, this was not the time to think of such things, so TTM let himself be swept away by the tide. He knew their efforts would be in vain, but it didn't matter. All he wanted to do was try to help save their city, and deep down, he was confident that Aargh would be there for the little girl. After all, Aargh had promised.

Carrying buckets of water and sand, a wave of people poured over the Once-Great Wall. Many others formed enormous miles-long lines, all the way to the river ports, passing buckets of water up Middling Street.

At that moment, there were no high or low homes, no lords or servants, no dockhands, or vendors. Everyone in Gemini City was the same, standing shoulder to shoulder, hand in hand, and supporting each other.

But would it be enough?

• • •

Thanks to Wrudge, Aargh's mind was free from the thoughts of the trees, but although his trusty familiar had given him the strength to clear his mind, there was no way Aargh was going to be able to calm his heart. He tried to concentrate with all of his might, but no answers came.

Aargh was in shock. He felt no scorching heat or painful embers burning into his robes. There was no Wizard of the Council or Master Prefect. Aargh felt only loneliness, emptiness, and darkness.

"I'm lost without him."

"I know. I'm sorry," a gentle voice soothed, but Aargh couldn't hear her through his grief and the growing rumble of the earth under their feet. He was alone, completely disconnected from the world. Lost.

The rumbling became overpowering, and Aargh looked up to see the Great Mount Ardilakk split in two before his very eyes. All at once, he broke through the haze that filled his heart and mind.

"Enough!" he heard himself scream. "Enough!"

With the loss of Wrudge, Aargh didn't even feel like a whole person anymore, but he knew that he had to get hold of himself. That meant coming up with a plan.

"Step one," Aargh thought, trying to concentrate, "Stop the forest from burning," but something distracted him.

It was still the feeling of loss but not only because of Wrudge. Something else was leaving him, too. Was he that connected to the forest? He knew that it was true. He could feel the loss of each tree, one by one, succumbing to the fire, and yet, he still stood there doing nothing!

Agony threatened to overtake Aargh once more. Then, something reached him through his hopelessness, a tiny voice calling out in the night. What was that? What did it say? He tried to focus on it.

"Papa?"

"Carya ovata!" Aargh exclaimed. "There's a child lost in the blaze!"

Frantically, Aargh searched, but it was too chaotic. People were running every which way. Carriages were crashing to the ground. Buildings were collapsing, and all of it was lit, bright as day, by the fire that blazed around them. How could he possibly find anything in this, let alone a lost child? And where was his Little One? He'd lost track of her when the trees started calling to the wizards. As far as he could tell, he was the only wizard left standing, thanks to Wrudge.

"Where are you, Little One?" he cried out. "I can't find you!"

"I'm right here, Papa," a small voice responded.

Wait, was she speaking to him?

A new realization dawned on Aargh that he hadn't even considered before. He was a papa! He wasn't just taking care of his Little One; he was her father now, and although this thought should have filled him with joy, all he felt was dread.

What kind of a father would allow this to happen to their child? He was a complete and utter failure! He hadn't stopped the imposter from destroying their world. He'd let it happen. Never again would he refer to himself as *le Grand* or tell people he was great. Never again would he wear over-sized robes or bow with an air of superiority. From this moment on, his title would be *Papa,* but Aargh didn't believe in himself. He wasn't sure if he was up to the challenge of something so important.

Aargh felt the weight of that responsibility and, once again, found himself with no answers, but something was different this time. There was something new. It was distant–just out of reach; not yet attainable but there nevertheless. For the first time, Aargh felt hope.

"Papa. Can you hear me? The fire is hungry," the voice interjected into his thoughts.

"What?"

Aargh was finally back in the here and now, but he didn't comprehend what she was saying.

"Papa. The fire is hungry. You need to feed it."

"Little One, I don't understand. Are you able to speak with the fire?"

"Yes. Of course, silly. So can you."

"No, I can't hear it. I can only speak to trees."

"Oh, Papa. Yes, you can. You can speak to anything you want to. All you have to do is try."

Aargh was stunned by the simplicity of this thought. But how? He'd spent a lifetime learning to speak with trees. Could it be that simple? Was it possible that the only reason he hadn't spoken to anything else was that he'd never tried? If *he* could speak, and if the *trees* could speak, why couldn't all living things speak? And fire was undoubtedly alive! He'd never seen anything filled with so much life as a rampaging fire.

Then, Aargh remembered. For the first time since becoming a student at the Gemini City School of Wizarding, Aargh remembered something from before he'd started writing in his diary. He remembered the fire.

"Papa! Papa, where are you?" little Aargh called out.

Aargh lived north of the Once-Great Wall on a farm his father had built for them. After the Lady of the House had passed, Lord Bardelthlain (the 13th Lord of Marble House) had found no joy in the grandeur of Upper Middling Street anymore. Keeping up appearances felt like a meaningless charade. So he'd decided to give it all up for a simpler life in the country with his newborn son. Together, they lived off the land and were happy until the day of the fire.

That night, Aargh had been roused by his father's yells.

"Get out of the house! Aargh, hurry!"

Choking on the smoke, Aargh had crawled out of a window and fallen to the ground, gasping for air. Propping himself up on his hands and knees, he'd watched as his father first made sure he was okay and then ran into the barn to save the horse. Shakily getting to his feet, Aargh had tried to get to his father, but it was no use. The fire was too hot. He shielded his eyes from the heat, and as he stood there watching, the roof of the barn collapsed. Through his tears, Aargh saw a tall man in long purple robes materialize out of the flames.

He approached the young boy and said, "I'm sorry, young Aargh. There was nothing I could do. My name is Aldenthwaine, Wizard of the Spire, and it's time for you to return to the city. Please, come with me."

Aargh looked at her delicate face, and it reminded him of his father, and of his friendship with Wrudge, and of the kindness Aldenthwaine had shown him as a young boy. As he looked at her, the mist that had clouded his mind finally lifted. To his dismay, he realized what he was supposed to ask her. He'd never asked what her name was. How was that possible? How could he have overlooked such a simple thing? Where was *his* kindness?

Ashamed, Aargh plucked up his courage and said, "I'm so sorry Little One."

"About what?"

"I must ask you a question. I have no idea why I haven't asked you this before, but I can't go another moment without knowing."

"Okay, Papa."

"Please forgive me, but I never asked what your name is. Would you please tell me?"

"What do you mean?"

"Your name? By what are you called?"

For the first time, a darkness came over the child. Aargh could feel the unbearable heat of the fire singeing the hairs on his arm. Something was wrong.

"But Papa, you know my name. You gave it to me. Don't you remember?"

The wizard was lost. What did she mean? When had he given her a name? The heat grew more intense, and the light in the child's eyes seemed to dim even more.

"I thought my name was *Mine*. Isn't that what you told me? 'You're *Mine*.' Isn't that who I am?"

Aargh felt both pain and joy at that moment.

"Oh, yes. You're most definitely, forever and always, without any question whatsoever, *Mine* and I am *Yours*."

She jumped into his arms, and the pain and heat of the fire faded like a distant memory.

"Would you like to speak to the fire now, Papa?" she whispered in his ear.

"Yes, please. Will you teach me?" Aargh whispered back to his daughter.

"Yes, Papa."

Hand in hand, they stared deep into the fire as ashes rained down around them. Suddenly, Aargh could hear the fire roaring. It was terrifying! Its voice was nothing like the ramblings of the trees. It was ravenous. It had to feed. There was no thought behind it. It didn't know what it wanted. The fire would eat anything! Then Aargh understood.

"Little One, we must feed the fire."

"Yes, Papa."

"We must feed the fire water."

"Yes, Papa."

"But there is no water. The fire has made the world dry. The earth is dry, and the air is dry."

"Silly Papa," she giggled. "There's always water. How else could the trees grow?"

"But I don't know the spell."

"Yes, you do. You have the spell right there in your book."

"What, this?" Aargh questioned, producing the *Book of Spell* from under his robes. "Useless! Completely useless! It only contains one spell, and that's for talking to trees."

Aargh cast the *Book of Spell* to the ground in disgust. Once proud of the fine leather-bound book, now it only served as a reminder of how much he'd lost and didn't understand.

"Besides, I can't do magic without Wrudge," he lamented. "A wizard is only as strong as the bond with his familiar."

"But Papa, Wrudge is still with you."

"Yes, Little One, he'll always be with me. I'll never forget him as long as I live."

"No, I mean, he's with you now. He's right there, in your *Book of Spells,*" she insisted.

Hesitantly, Aargh reached into his robes, producing another book–an old, worn, leather-bound book. The pages of that well-loved book had been turned many times by the wizard. Now he puzzled over it.

"This? This is my diary," he said quizzically. "It doesn't contain any spells."

"Oh, Papa! Of course, it does. It contains stories, the most powerful spells in the world. Every tree knows that!"

Aargh knew in his heart that she was speaking the truth. And the most powerful story of them all? The story a parent reads to their child.

Aargh looked at the unassuming book with a mixture of awe and sorrow. So many memories were carefully remembered on those pages, and although he'd opened its cover countless times to write in it over the years, he'd never once thought about reading a story back out of it. Aargh wondered what that would feel like, especially now.

"Read me a story, Papa."

Gingerly, Aargh opened the book, letting it fall open to a page of its choosing. He looked at the page, smiled to himself, and began, "Silly old Wrudge got stuck in a can today," and the pair stepped directly into the fire.

Chapter 11

THE SAPLING

Lazy leaves drifted on currents of warm air like long, winding rivers in the sky. The sun sparkled between them, dappling the ground as they passed. One leaf slipped out of the stream and ever so gently floated down, landing on Aargh's upturned face. Absently, he brushed it away. It was tickling his nose, and he didn't want to get up yet. He rolled over, scrunching his eyes against the bright summer sunlight.

"Why is my bed so hard this morning?" he wondered dreamily and then sat straight up, shaking the sleep from his mind. They'd done it! They'd saved Mother Tree from the fire!

Aargh had spoken to the water, its flowing thoughts long and sinewy in his mind, and it had agreed to sacrifice itself to save the tree. Of course, water is blessed with reincarnation, so someday it would rejoin the rivers when it fell back down from the heavens. Still, it was a noble sacrifice, nevertheless. The last thing Aargh remembered was a tremendous whoosh and a cloud of steam rising all around them. Then, completely exhausted, he'd collapsed onto the charred ground, passing out from the exertion.

As Aargh looked around, he saw the skeletons of countless trees poking like spines out of the smoldering wasteland. Many lay like fallen heroes on the scorched earth, black and lifeless. All of her children had been destroyed, but together, they'd saved her, the last tree in the forest.

Aargh rubbed his bloodshot eyes and looked up. His daughter was standing with her hands on Mother Tree's trunk. Deep in thought, her eyes were closed, and she was breathing very slowly. As the smoke and steam parted, a lump rose in Aargh's throat. Mother Tree's right side was singed and desiccated. Gone was the lush beauty of her green crown. So different from the first time he'd met her.

Aargh and the other novices were brought into the forest to meet Mother Tree on their first field trip. One by one, they'd been presented to her. Aargh remembered bowing low and saying, "It's lovely to meet you," not knowing if she would reply. She didn't. That would come later.

At the time, Aargh didn't understand what was going on or why they were there, but being near her made him feel happy. So whenever he could, he'd steal away and visit the glade where she stood.

Being the oldest and wisest tree in the forest, he often wondered why she talked to him (especially considering the frivolous things that concerned his young mind), but she did, and they became fast friends. Many a wonderful hour had been passed nestled in the embrace of her strong roots, trading stories in the warm afternoon sun.

Now, Aargh looked on his friend with profound sadness. She was suffering, of that he was sure, but he didn't know how to help her. He welcomed the interruption from his dark thoughts when a little hand slipped in his, but what he heard didn't comfort him.

"The Wizard of the Council made his wand from one of her branches," she said, pointing to the blackened arms.

"I don't understand. Magic only resides in living things. A broken branch wouldn't work."

"His wand *was* alive. If you take a branch from a tree, it dies, but if a tree gives a branch to you, it lives on."

"But why? Why would Mother Tree do such a thing?" Aargh asked, unable to understand why Mother Tree would give away something so sacred, especially to the Wizard of the Council.

"Because she had to. Mother Tree knew she was dying, and she needed someone to watch over her children. Since the Wizard of the Council hadn't ever been presented to her, she couldn't see through his magic. She only saw a reflection of her own selflessness. Mother Tree offered her bough, so he could use what strength she had left to care for her children. But once she gave it to him, he betrayed her and used the wand to make himself powerful."

The false wizard's deceit weighed heavily on Aargh's mind.

"Is this what had happened all those centuries ago, when something laid waste to the northern cities?" he wondered to himself. "If not a deranged wizard, then what could have caused such devastation?"

Aldenthwaine was right. Magic was far too dangerous to allow it to fall into the wrong hands. Aargh would have to figure out how to hide this new knowledge from those who would abuse the power, but that was for later. Right now, he needed to help Mother Tree and restore the forest, but how?

No matter how hard he tried, Mother Tree didn't answer him. At first, he thought she might be too tired, or maybe she didn't trust him anymore? No, that wasn't it. She was too quiet. It was like she wasn't even there. Slowly and methodically, he followed her roots. Still, there was no answer. Aargh started to go deeper.

"Where is she?" he wondered.

Aargh was so focused on the task that he didn't realize how deep he was going. Somewhere in the back of his mind, Aargh began to wonder if he'd be able to find his way back out, but on he went. Deeper and deeper, he burrowed with his mind. No root was too small. No root was too long. He would find the end, and she would be there. She had to be. She must be hiding down here somewhere. Still, she didn't answer.

Aargh began to shiver. He'd heard stories of wizards burrowing so deeply that they ceased to exist in the natural world. Would that be his fate? Was he destined to vanish from the world and become the roots of history? Then a new thought occurred to him.

"Could it be possible?" Aargh asked himself.

Aargh had always referred to himself as *great* but was he? He doubted. Well, no. It wasn't so much doubt as humility. Aargh had become humbled before the magnitude of the world but here, surrounded by the desolation wrought by the imposter, he had to try.

With that, Aargh did something no wizard had ever dared to do before. He spoke to the earth itself.

It was overwhelming. In the center of his body, Aargh felt the deep, dark rumble of her enormous voice. For a terrifying moment, he was convinced it would tear him apart.

Aargh reflexively pulled his mind back, but no, he couldn't stop now. He had to speak with her. And if this was to be his final act, he was going to make it count!

Aargh pleaded with her, but no answers came. Again and again, he asked, but it was no use. He could tell she was speaking to him, but Aargh couldn't comprehend what she was saying.

In his mind, that familiar voice once again whispered gently to him.

"Papa," the voice said. "She's there, but she doesn't move as quickly as you or me. Be patient. Be calm."

The sound of that little voice eased his mind, and the panic drained from his heart. As his thoughts began to clear, the most wondrous thing happened.

"Oh, Platanus occidentalis! I can understand her. I can understand the Earth Mother!" he rejoiced.

Aargh let go, allowing the Earth Mother's knowledge to flow into him and overflow around him. It felt as if his mind was spreading out like ripples on the surface of the water–his thoughts traveling in every direction at once. Although Aargh wished he could stay there basking in the warmth of her knowledge, he knew time was running out for Mother Tree. So he reined in his thoughts, focusing on the one question he had to ask.

"Great Earth Mother, please, grant me the wisdom and knowledge to save Mother Tree."

There was a long pause, and when the Earth Mother finally responded, her answer filled him with anguish.

"I cannot," she said. "Nothing lives forever. All things that live above must return to the earth below. It is the way of the Great Cycle."

Aargh couldn't believe what he was hearing. Mother Tree stood dying right in front of him, and he could do nothing? His daughter would never play in the fallen leaves of autumn again or lay on a bed of soft pine needles. Aargh couldn't bear the thought of raising her in a world without trees. Then the Earth Mother's wise voice came again, and he tried to listen through his sorrow.

"Mother Tree did not give only one branch. She gave two but kept the second disguised, hidden from the Wizard of the Council."

A small glimmer of hope began to grow in Aargh's heart.

"Find the One True Root and follow it to the very end," the Earth Mother instructed. "There, you will find a tiny sapling. If you nourish it and help it to grow, the people of Gemini City will once again know the beauty of trees."

With newfound purpose, Aargh clawed his way back to the world. History flooded over him, threatening to wash him away forever, but he doggedly focused on his mission to find the last sapling. With a rush, he exploded back into his body and flung himself to the ground.

He scrabbled and scratched–darted and raced. He would follow the One True Root to its end, but…but…he couldn't find it! Had he taken a wrong turn? Back he went and started over. No luck. Again and again he began, growing ever more frantic as he searched for the sapling.

Aargh's once-loved robes lay in ruins around him, torn and blackened by the scorched earth. He didn't care. Aargh's hat lay abandoned on the ground, and his fingernails were caked with dirt, but he didn't care about that either. With the ferocity of a wild animal, he threw himself into every nook and crevice, but his heart was too filled with love, and his mind too filled with emotion, to see the future clearly. Nevertheless, on he went. He took every branch and examined every tendril. He would find the end. He would find the sapling. He would—

"Papa?"

"Yes, Little One?" Aargh responded absently, as parents sometimes do when they're focusing on something else.

"What are you looking for?"

"I'm searching for Mother Tree's sapling."

"Papa?"

"Yes."

"I am here."

And everything became clear to him. The knowledge didn't make him feel powerful or superior the way he'd always dreamed it would. It made him feel blessed with understanding because isn't that what we all hope for, to understand why things happen to us?

Good or bad, difficult or easy, the question that lies in our hearts is *why?* Only one person in the entire world knew the answer to that question, and interestingly enough, he didn't care anymore. Not at all.

"Why?" seemed like such a silly question. Aargh didn't care about *why;* he only cared about *who.* And as he looked at his daughter, with a love that filled him so fully that he couldn't keep it inside, he began to cry. He cried tears of joy and tears of sorrow. He cried because the world had been lost but was once again found. He cried because no other thing he could have done would have felt so right.

"Papa."

"Yes, Little One."

"You're watering the earth," she mused.

"Will it help the trees to grow?" he asked, with a smile that reached his eyes.

"It already has."

All around them and as far as they could see, leaves had begun to peek out of the earth, turning the black forest floor into a lovely carpet of green.

"You truly are a child of the trees, aren't you?" he asked rhetorically.

The sapling smiled and reached out her hand.

"Can we go home, now?"

"Yes, it's time to go home."

Epilogue

A LITTLE COTTAGE IN THE WOODS

Thrundsday the 39th

"Today, we plant this tree in honor of Wrudge. Rat. Familiar. Friend. And, in accordance with the tradition of our city, we'll tell the tree a story to help its first root grow. May it be the first of many roots as it records our family's history and the magical world around us.

"We've thought long and hard about which story to share on this special day. Wrudge and I knew each other for years, and we had many grand adventures. However, there's one adventure that stood out above all the rest–a true testament to his loyalty, cunning, and deep, abiding love of food.

"And so, our story begins on a day much like today, a fine summer's morn exactly one year ago as we strolled up Middling Street. It's a tale about a magnificent home, a daring escape, a special girl, and of course, roast lamb."

As is often the case, one story turned into many, and they sat with the tree all afternoon. Aargh told stories about their days at the wizarding school, of an exciting winter break when they had followed the high pass to see the frozen falls, extravagant dinners in stately homes with their lords and ladies, and daring adventures on the piers that lined the River Wide. All wizards love to tell tales of their exploits, and Aargh was no exception.

When the sun began to dip below the horizon, they decided it was time to go in for some dinner (and maybe a mug of hot cocoa, too). There was a slight nip in the evening air and, well, any excuse to have a mug of cocoa!

The storytellers rubbed their legs and stretched their bodies. They'd been sitting for quite a while, and things weren't working as well as they should. Once they were up and brushed off, they turned to head inside. To Aargh's surprise, he noticed they weren't alone.

From under a nearby shrub, a small group of rats appeared. They were hesitant at first–only poking their noses out and sniffing the air–but after seeing Aargh's smile, they decided it was safe enough to come over.

"Well now, my little friends," Aargh said. "How long have you been there? Have you been listening to our stories, too?"

The rats nodded and asked, "May we tell the tree a story about Wrudge?"

Although it wasn't surprising that Wrudge had friends who would also want to pay their respects, Aargh was caught off guard by their request. He tried to reply but felt the words get stuck in his throat. In the end, he managed to get out, "We'd be delighted if you told the tree a story about dear Wrudge."

Then, to his amazement, the brush began to glow with many lights. As the rats emerged from the shadows, they formed a long line stretching as far as the eye could see, their glow shimmering in the dusky twilight.

In small groups, they came to share their stories. Some rats were solemn as they spoke, telling stories about how Wrudge helped them through a difficult time. Others chuckled to themselves or laughed out loud as they reminisced about a young—and often silly–Wrudge. Many told stories about Wrudge doing something for the *mischief.* Although this was a term given to the colony by people, the rats were rather fond of it. Mischief seemed fitting somehow, so they'd adopted it for their own.

All through the night, rats came to pay their respects, and by daybreak, the little tree had many roots, indeed.

• • •

One night, when Aargh was putting his daughter to bed, she looked at him and said, "I'd like to choose a name to honor Mother Tree."

"That sounds like a wonderful idea," he said, kissing her forehead.

The pair had spent much of the past year rebuilding the forest. They'd also ventured into town to help the people there, too, not that Geminians needed much help. They're a resilient bunch!

After the Great Fire, everyone had quickly set about rebuilding the city, and it was going well, too. The Stonemason's Guild, of which many Geminians were members, was even rebuilding the Once-Great Wall. This time, it had many grand archways that led into the northern forest. Everything about the city was changing, and although it would take time, things were getting better day by day.

Aargh was particularly fond of the tree and leaf engravings that now covered the once-smooth stone surfaces up and down Middling Street. But that wasn't the only change. After the position of Master Prefect was eliminated, committees of concerned Geminians started popping up to help guide the reconstruction of the city. It felt like everyone was participating. They even heard that the walls around Old Eastie Sowtown were being taken down. Aargh was looking forward to visiting there one day soon. Word was they were great farmers and had even dug a cranberry bog!

The rebuilding of the high homes on Upper Middling Street was going well, too, but not as dwellings for the wealthy. Now, they housed museums filled with historical artifacts and stories about the city (all but Marble House, which was left as a memorial).

Exactly one year after the Great Fire, a rededication ceremony was held in the Congregational House. Although there was still much work to be done, everyone was overjoyed to see all four hallways reopened. Aarghathlain, Wizard of the Spire, Historian and Keeper of the General Generations, Root-Reader of the First Order, and newly appointed Head of the Gemini City School of Wizarding, planted an oak tree sapling right in the middle of the Grand Rotunda. Everyone came to tell the tree their stories, and she grew strong with many roots.

Through it all, the little girl had waited. She wanted to meet as many trees as possible before choosing her mothername. In the end, it was a simple choice to make—its dark, pointed green leaves, delicate white flowers, and rich red berries that stood out against the white, snowy landscape seemed perfect. Yes, that had to be it, and now it was time to take its name for her own.

Although they often visited the Spire, Aargh and his daughter made their life together in the Northern Forest. They had a cozy cottage made of living trees, a babbling stream to dip their feet into on warm days, and even a small garden out back where they grew vegetables right in the ground! The pair took long walks in the forest and made many friends–the trees being as eager to hear their stories as to tell their own.

They even heard whispers of a wandering storyteller–a tall, slender man who wore outlandish clothes–traveling from town to town teaching children the history of Gemini City. People said he was the most knowledgeable person in the land, and he never left without saying, "If you learn nothing else from me, learn this: Pay attention to the world around you. It's a wondrous place, but only if you take the time to notice it."

• • •

As happy as those days were, nothing lasts forever, and one night, that gentle voice once again called to him.

"Papa, wake up!"

The sound of Holly-Mine's voice sent a chill through Aargh's body. It had been a long time since he'd heard her sound that way.

"Are you okay, Holly-Mine? What is it?"

"Papa, they're coming."

"I don't understand. Who's coming?" Aargh asked, dreading the answer.

"The Norters."

Glossary

alleyway. The space between the grand stone buildings of Gemini City. Generally considered private property or servant ways on the upper streets, alleyways are more the domain of rats than people. It would be unwise to find yourself in an alleyway on any of the southern blocks–especially late at night.

attik. A second-floor room (usually hidden) used to store old, unwanted, or unused items in the high homes and other affluent dwellings.

block. Delineated by sidestreets, blocks represent the smallest planned subdivision of the cities. Unlike the rest of the elders' designs, the layout of blocks was left to architects and homeowners–ostensibly to allow for creativity. The real reason was to permit the wealthiest members of high society to build their palatial homes without limitations.

Footman. The person charged with hanging wizards upside down by their feet as punishment for not doing their job properly.

Geminians. This term is used to describe everyone who lives in Gemini City except for Old Eastie Sowtown. Those residents are usually referred to as *outcasts* or *outers*. Interestingly, the people of Old Eastie Sowtown refer to themselves as *townies*.

happenny. The term for a half 'pentce–derived from the old Sowtown saying, *I found a happy penny.* It used to refer to any money found on the ground or that fell out of someone's pocket.

mischief. The term for a group of rats. Additionally, male rats are called bucks; unmated females, does; pregnant or parent females, dams; and infants are called kittens or pups.

'pentce. Derived from the vernacular, as in, "I spents good money on that!" Later it was adopted as the term for the smallest recognized denomination of money used in Gemini City though they are often cut in half (called a *happenny*).

street. By design, each of the four cities of the Quadropolis had four main thoroughfares called streets (two running north/south and two running east/west). Additionally, four streets separated the cities (Middle Building Streets North, South, East, and West). Middle Building Street South, now known as Middling Street, is the only separating street that still exists today. Middle Building Streets West and East were turned into the Once-Great Wall, and Middle Building Street North was lost when the northern cities burned. The woodland path that remains is called Old Middle-Forest Road, but it is seldom traveled in the modern day.

sidestreet. Each of the seventeen surviving squares contain six sidestreets (three running north/south and three running east/west). No one is sure what the roads look like, or if there are any at all, in Old Eastie Sowtown. It's rumored that their streets are not organized and might even be curved!

square. Meticulously planned out during the construction of the Quadropolis, the four cities contained nine squares, each comprised of sixteen blocks. Seventeen of these squares have survived to the modern-day (the eighteenth having been walled off and no longer traveled by Geminians).

Sundsday. Originally Suds Day, or the day of cleaning, Sundsday is one of the nine days of the week: Mundsday, Toodlesday, Wendingsday, Landingsday, Middlingsday, Thrundsday, Frittersday, Sattersday, and Sundsday.

Exclamations

Excerpt from

A TREE BY ANY OTHER NAME...

Second Year Lecture #733

by

Aarghathlain, Wizard of the Spire

Carya ovata, commonly known as shagbark hickory, is a large, deciduous tree that can grow to over 100 feet in height. It can live more than 350 years and produces an edible nut that has a sweet taste.

Platanus occidentalis, commonly known as water beech, buttonwood, and many other names (including sycamore), can grow to heights of 150 feet or more and are often divided near the ground into several secondary trunks. Interestingly, the trunks of large trees are often hollow. Leaf petioles usually grow below a tree's buds; however, the sycamore's petioles practically surround their leaf buds, hiding them from view.

Quercus macrocarpa, commonly known as bur oak or mossycup oak, is one of the most majestic-looking oaks. It is a deciduous tree of the white oak group that typically grows 60 to 80 feet in height. At the top, it has a broad-spreading, rounded crown. Its acorn cups are covered with a mossy scale, or bur, near the rim.

Quercus rubra, commonly known as red oak or northern red oak, is a deciduous tree with a broad-spreading irregular crown. This oak generally grows to a height of 50 to 75 feet and has dark, lustrous green leaves with toothed lobes.

THE WIZARD'S DIARY SERIES

BOOK 1

THE WIZARD'S DIARY

Magic comes to Gemini City.

BOOK 2

THE SWORD GUILDEBRANDE

The journey to Ardilakk begins.

SHORT STORIES

THE ANCIENT QUADROPOLIS

TTM's lecture on the steps of the Congregational House.

THE ADVENTURE CONTINUES!

for more information, please visit:

www.wizardsdiary.com

Made in the USA
Middletown, DE
12 December 2021